KU-499-986

PENGUIN BOOKS

THE HARPOLE REPORT

J. L. Carr is a Kettering publisher of standard poets, idiosyncratic maps and unlikely dictionaries. He is also the author of several novels including *A Day in Summer* (1964), *A Season in Sinji* (1967), *How Steeple Sinderby Wanderers Won the FA Cup* (1975) and *A Month in the Country* (Penguin, 1980), which won the *Guardian* Fiction Prize for 1980 and was nominated for the 1980 Booker McConnell Prize.

J. L. CARR

The Harpole Report

PENGUIN BOOKS

Penguin Books Ltd Harmondsworth, Middlesex, England
Viking Penguin Inc., 40 West 23rd Street, New York, New York 10010, U.S.A.
Penguin Books Australia Ltd, Ringwood, Victoria, Australia
Penguin Books Canada Ltd, 2801 John Street, Markham, Ontario, Canada L3R 1B4
Penguin Books (N.Z.) Ltd, 182 190 Wairau Road, Auckland 10, New Zealand

First published by Martin Secker & Warburg Ltd 1972
Published in Penguin Books 1984
Reprinted 1984 (twice), 1985

Printed in Great Britain by
Richard Clay (The Chaucer Press) Ltd,
Bungay Suffolk

FOR SALLY

THE HARPOLE REPORT

'The fourth subject is the most important – the teachers themselves. They *are* education, and yet very little is systematically known about them. Almost any additional knowledge will be welcome ...

'Who are these people prepared to devote themselves to education? Why did they take it up and what happens when they do?

'... Nor is much known about how, in detail, teachers spend their time when they are established. The "Natural History" of the school still awaits its Gilbert White ... I expect that the most rewarding research in the next quarter of a century will be anthropological in inspiration – small-scale intensive studies of individual schools and classrooms and the richness of human relationship within them.'

Michael Young
Founder of the magazines *WHERE?* and *WHICH?*

(Reproduced by kind permission of the author, and Routledge & Kegan Paul Ltd)

> *'It is the death of the spirit we must fear. To believe only what one is taught and brought up to believe, to repeat what one has been told to say, to do only what one is expected to do, to live like a factory-made doll, to lose confidence in one's independence and the hope of better things – that is the death of the spirit.'*
> *Tokutomi Roka*

1

Having been commissioned to make this independent report on what happened to Mr. G. Harpole, I should like it immediately made clear that it was Harpole himself who asked that I – as an older, more experienced headmaster – should comment on this last term which ended his career.

He has allowed me to see his 'journal' (a private work-diary), and has shown me relevant items of correspondence. Although, predictably, I was refused access to the Local Education Authority's files, I have been able to use carbons, which Harpole retained, of all his business and personal letters and have made some incidents more intelligible by extracts from the official school log and from diaries written by very young children as daily exercises in composition. Thus, by and large, everyone speaks for himself.

It has not been a task of my choosing, but there has been one worthwhile compensation. As I have put this business into some sort of order, my sympathy and admiration has warmed not only to several of those caught up in it but to others unknown to me; isolated little bands, here and there clinging to scarcely tenable positions amidst the dust of battle in the front lines of English Education.

And remember this. A school is a most complex institution. Children and teachers, administrators and their minor officials, caretakers, cooks, medical officers, government inspectors, governors. And parents. All these grinding away, in and out of mesh. Is there any wonder then that sometimes – as in this case of Harpole – there is a terrifying jarring of gears or, worse still, that unforgettable coffin-thump of a big-end gone?

ARTHUR S. CHADBAND, F.R.I.H., F.R.H.S., HEAD-
MASTER OF TAMPLING ST. NICHOLAS C.E. (AIDED)
PRIMARY (J) SCHOOL, TO P. TUSKER, B.SC.,
ASSISTANT EDUCATION OFFICER

Referring to your communication of the 4th inst., allow me to
allay your disquiet about difficulties likely to arise at Tampling
St. Nicholas C.E. (Aided) Primary School during the few weeks
leave-of-absence which the County Education Committee and
my Managers, assisted by your own good offices, have graciously
granted me.

Although Mr. Harpole is but in his early thirties, I adjudge
him to be a most reliable, conscientious and painstaking
employee of the Education Committee. He has had outstanding success with the Scholarship Class. In fact, our Eleven
Plus Successes are much in excess of the County's average, often
by as much as twenty percentum.

However, I am in accord with your belief that there are
grounds for fearing insubordination when one member of a
staff is singled out for elevation to a position of internal
authority. But as you will recall during our confidential chat
(which, incidentally, was much valued by me), the only obstruc-
tive element in my school is Mrs. Grindle-Jones who, I regret to
report, still harbours resentment at being passed over when we
appointed Mr. Harpole to the vacant Graded Post of Responsibility Scale One. Nevertheless, my conscience, (as I re-iterated at
the time) is clear, and I am grateful that my Managers came
round to my way of thinking that it would have been improper
for the wife of a neighbouring Headmaster to have had access to
confidential documents during my temporary absence.

Finally, be assured that I shall maintain close links of communication with my school. I have made it clear to Mr. Harpole
that my experience during thirty-three years as Head of
Tampling St. Nicholas will be at his instant call.

I trust that you, your good wife and the two children, enjoyed
a beneficent health-giving vacation in the Isle of Man.

*It is plain from Chadband's excessive gratitude and his effort to
foster a more personal relationship by his reference to the Tusker
Family's holiday that he is uneasy, fearful that his escape to a*

2

South-Coast resort might yet be blocked. Although ostensibly about Harpole, this letter is to remind Tusker that Tampling St. Nicholas C.E. (Aided) School is a diamond in the Local Authority's crown. It would appear that by streaming, coaching and cleverly forecasting examination papers, Chadband has built a formidable reputation for filching grammar-school places from deserving children in neighbouring schools.

OFFICIAL LOG-BOOK

I, Mr. (George) Harpole, Certificated Assistant (P.O.R.Grade One), to-day assumed charge of this school during the temporary absence in the furtherance of Professional Studies of its Headmaster, Mr. A. S. Chadband, F.R.I.H., F.R.H.S.
The Staff is as follows:

Class Four – Emma *Foxberrow*, M.A. (Cantab.)	Graduate (Untrained) (Supply)
Class Three – (Mrs.) Rita *Grindle-Jones*	Certificated Assistant
Class Two – *Pintle*, James Albert	Certificated Assistant
Class One – *Croser*, Sidney	Certificated Assistant (on probation)
The Backward Class – Grace *Tollemache*	Unqualified Assistant
Mr. Edwin Ezra *Theaker*	Caretaker

JOURNAL

My first day as Acting Head of our school. To my chagrin nothing required my attention. Am already aware how much I shall miss the bustle of classroom teaching and hope that the work in the Scholarship Class does not suffer. The Office has been very reticent about the Supply they have sent us, (a university graduate – which usually foreshadows either the collapse of discipline or primitive instruction, i.e. 'Open-your-exercise-books-and-take-down-these-notes-I-took-down-x-years-ago'). I shall find time to keep a fatherly eye on her.

However, filled in the day usefully by rearranging the contents

3

of Mr. Chadband's desk drawers, placing the new studio colour-photo of Edith in my stationery drawer so that I see her whenever I need notepaper or an envelope. I temporarily put away Mr. Chadband's Certificate of the Institute of Hygiene and replaced it with my framed manuscript copy (on vellum) of Sir H. Newbolt's great poem, *Vitai Lampada*, which I did for Art at College. The lines I find particularly inspiring are,

> 'The sand of the desert is sodden red. . . .
> The Gatling's jammed and the Colonel dead,
> The River of Death has brimmed his banks,
> But the voice of a schoolboy rallies the ranks:
> "Play up! Play up! and play the game!" '

Took my first service in Morning Assembly, selecting the hymns, 'Fair wav'd the golden corn in Canaan's Pleasant Land' and 'Forth in Thy Name O Lord I go my daily labours to pursue'. I was disappointed to note that our new member of staff did not join in our singing until the line;

> 'Preserve me from my calling's snare'

which she suddenly sang in an excessively loud voice and then ceased. The children were so astonished that they too ceased singing and stared at her with undisguised curiosity.

I find Mrs. Grindle-Jones very heavy on the loud pedal which she keeps permanently depressed and also find it irritating that, after three years, she still plays the 'Hyacinth Waltz' for the children to march in and out to. Not only has the music ceased to have aesthetic significance, but it is most difficult to keep step in three-time.

Just after home-time, Mr. Tusker, B.Sc., called in and asked if everything was well with us. I assured him that he could rely on me to keep work proceeding smoothly until my Headmaster's resumption. As he went, he paused and said significantly, 'At the Office, we are watching this term at Tampling St. Nicholas with the greatest attention, Harpole.'

This is promising. Harpole does well to keep official entries in the School's Log brief and factual. Although secured with a built-in lock against the casual reader, this log belongs to his employers and anything recorded can be used either by them against Harpole

4

or against the Local Authority by counsel for litigious parents. Because the pages are numbered Harpole will not be able to remove injudicious entries. Thus, when recording controversial events he will be wise to discreetly weight them in his own favour.

It is significant that he has converted Chadband's 'My' to 'Our' school and that he gives thought to the selection of hymns. However, we must hope that he advances to more sophisticated selection, choosing an occasional Christmas carol in summer and 'Summer Suns are Glowing' in mid-winter. Not only do children enjoy unpredictability but it will warn his staff that a streak of eccentricity lurks and that he must not be taken too much for granted.

2

A modest innovation. Having long been of the opinion that we English are unduly reticent in love of our country, I instructed the caretaker, Mr. Theaker, to hoist the Union Jack on the flagstaff at 8.50 each morning. Not only will this foster patriotism but, as the flag will be visible from a great distance, it will warn laggards to hasten.

Mr. Theaker pretended not to hear when I gave him this order and, when I repeated it, said that the flag 'was wore out', 'the sea air had rotted it' and it had 'gone to the Tip'. I immediately sent off a requisition-form to the Office asking that a new flag should be supplied.

TUSKER TO HARPOLE

My Clerk informs me that a National Flag was supplied to your school immediately before the visit by the Chairman of the County Council seven years ago. With normal usage and care this item of equipment should still be in serviceable condition and I should be grateful if you will kindly inform me of the circumstances attendant on your need for a second flag.

THEAKER TO HARPOLE (Left on desk.)

I have brought up what you said about it being my job to put up the flag each and every morning and the caretaker union is taking it up with the Education so as we know what our job is and isn't.

(unsigned)

I was called upon to-day by the industrial disputes officer of the Transport and General Workers' Union, complaining that you have instructed your caretaker, Mr. E. E. Theaker, to hoist a flag each morning.

I would point out that the Local Education Committee has laid down that the principal duties of its caretakers are to maintain (*a*) Heat (*b*) Cleanliness (*c*) Security, and that Other Duties should only be undertaken when and if time permits. In view of this, no doubt you would like to re-consider the ill-considered position you have taken up, and I shall expect to hear what course of action in this vexatious matter you propose to take.

I note that you have not yet informed me why you require a second flag.

JOURNAL

Feel downcast and dispirited. Cancelled the daily ceremony of Hoisting the Flag as it has only brought me a parcel of trouble. Wrote to the Office saying that the original flag has now been found in excellent condition, and that I have cancelled the request made to Theaker.

Harpole has not covered himself with glory in his Fight for the Flag. Basically, it was a good idea and would have added a touch of gaiety which would have pleased the children. By retreating, he has lost face with everyone. It is unaccountable that he failed to notice that, though Tusker has not greeted news of Harpole's instructions to his caretaker with wild applause, neither has he directly censured him. Plainly this education officer knows that patriotism, like religion, is charmed ground on which only fools tread firmly.

JOURNAL

Immensely cheered by visit from Lucinda Bull's father who is a scrap merchant. He said 'as how hearing the kids wasn't going to get a flag we could have this one as he'd won it when they had him in the Army.'

I readily accepted this, assuming his generosity to be disinterested. I was in error because he went on to say that his wife had asked how long Lucinda was going to be in 'The Backwards', as one or two of the other 'kids' had been 'twitting' her. I assured him that he need not feel concern because, in Class 2X, Lucinda could proceed happily at her own pace.

This did not appear to reassure him and he kept asking what they had to do to 'get her out of it' and that, if I would tell him, he and his 'Missus' would get her extra 'tutoring'. I was at a loss for an answer because a child does not 'get out' of 2X (The Backward Class) until it leaves to join Form 1.C. (The Backward Form) in the Sec. Mod.

When he had gone, Titus Fawcett from Class 4 entered and said that he had heard we had been given a flag and that he would like to hoist it daily. He went on to say that there was no need to demonstrate how to do it because the new teacher, Miss Foxberrow, had shown him, she having been a Girl Guide and knowing knots.

NOTE FROM HARPOLE CIRCULATED TO TEACHING STAFF

I feel confident of your support for the two trifling procedural deviations in routine I propose making.
1 All male staff should cease insistence on being addressed as 'Sir'. This archaic title inhibits easy relationship between ourselves and the children. Although they accept it as The Way of Things in schools, it implies that we are different from other men. Similarly female staff should discourage children from addressing them as 'Miss', 'Teacher' or 'Ma'am'.
2 After reading an instructive article in this week's *Teacher*, I propose to dispense with the use of the cane and expect any colleagues, who may *unofficially* employ it, to follow suit. I cannot imagine anything more likely to permanently damage teacher/child/parent relationship.

Harpole seems to have learned little from his Fight for the Flag.

'Trifling procedural deviations' is a truly awesome understatement. In a school run along the lines which were the height of fashion when Chadband was trained in the 20s by men who learnt their educational practice in the early years of the century, such changes as Harpole proposes amount to revolution in all its naked terror.

Here Harpole could have learned discretion from Tusker and not compromised in writing. Far better that he should have waited until the tide was running in his favour, and then brought forward his ideas over a cup of tea in the staff-room.

And he should know better than do several education committees who advertise for female *teachers as though buying biological specimens.*

2X, 'The Backwards'? Surely, if Mr. Bull, a scrap merchant, has seen through this clumsy, belittling practice, Harpole, the professional, cannot sustain it . . .

PINTLE TO HARPOLE (note by hand)

My class and all children with whom I come in contact will continue to address me as 'Sir'. All strikes, demonstrations, civil disturbances, pornographic theatrical performances and bedding without wedding are due to such erosion of the social order.

I am one of the *Old School* and refuse to bow before the rising tide of National Decay. I shall disregard your notice and shall bring this matter to the notice of my employers, requesting them to furnish me with a ruling on your action.

JOURNAL

. . . hurried round to Pintle's room and assured him that my circular was meant only as a suggestion and that, if he felt so strongly about this trifling change, he should disregard it. I further hoped to mollify him by the assurance that I respected a man who spoke his mind and suggested we forget the matter. However, I told him that, for my part, I was finished with the cane and this I should tell the children during a future assembly.

Whilst cycling to my first net of the season met our new member of staff, Miss Foxberrow. She appeared to be wearing a

voluminous plaid cloak but further examination was prevented
by my cricket bag catching in the handlebars causing me to fall
off. Postponed practising at the nets until next week.

ALEXANDER FESTING, ESQ., TO HARPOLE

My daughter Martha informs me of your announcement to the
children that you do not possess a cane. I urge you to reconsider
this. Living as I do on the Muttler Council Estate, I continually
am apprised of multiplying acts of the utmost depravity resultant
from the Permissive Society fostered by the *so-called* Government of the Country and the sloppy punishments awarded by
our *so-called* Courts of Law.

I can declare with the utmost conviction as a Scot that it was
the whippings with the tawse I received at school and from a
God-fearing father at home that saved me from the deterioration
into animality which sullies adolescence in the male sex. It is
regrettable enough that severe birchings of adults are no longer
administered, but it is going too far to remove the fear of
chastisement from our children.

I trust you will reconsider your decision.

HARPOLE TO FESTING

Much as I respect your feelings in this matter I am afraid that I
cannot agree that the cane is a lasting solution to anything. I
agree that it appears to effect a swift remedy but, in my experience, it only causes the dust to be swept beneath the carpet –
and usually someone else's carpet. Indeed an Expert in Yorkshire
believes that the incidence of juvenile crimes of violence is much
higher in areas served by caning-schools.

Thank you for writing to me as I value the interest of parents
in our school.

*One of Harpole's virtues appears to be his prompt and reasonable
answer to parental letters. This is not so common as one might
suppose. In fact, some heads do not reply at all to letters from*

10

parents – for reasons ranging through idleness and clerical disorg-
anization to resentment that the correspondent does not immedi-
ately concede the principle of almost divine infallibility. And there
is the occasional monster who not only does not reply but immedi-
ately arraigns the correspondent's wretched child and browbeats
it, so that other parents are besought by terrified children never to
write letters except in terms of slavish adulation.

HARPOLE TO EDITH WARDLE

. . . my heart sank when Mrs. Teale, my landlady, asked me to
find a home for yet another of her confounded kittens. Honestly
it is too bad of her taking advantage of me working in a school.
And it is getting harder and harder to get rid of them as I have
had to place eight since autumn, and children have been for-
bidden by many parents to accept them even as prizes. This
particular one was a fine marmalade male with a bold, confident
look and, for once, I reluctantly approved of the arty name she
had bestowed on it – 'Glorious Apollo'!

Anyway I managed to pass it off on the Gaskins who live on
the Muttler Estate. A few days later I asked Polly Gaskin how
Apollo was getting on. 'Oh, he is called Fluff now,' she said.
'Mum said he thought too much of hisself like Dad's brother
Fred, so she took him to the vet and had him attended to.'

3

The Eleven-Plus results came in this morning's post but decided not to announce these in assembly as was Mr. Chadband's custom. Instead, I hurriedly duplicated a letter to all parents of the candidates informing them that the Education Committee had decided which was the most suitable school for their child and informed them which – Melchester Grammar, Melchester High or Melchester Sec. Mod. However, most of the children secretly slit their envelopes and, as I was passing the cloakrooms, I saw that Daphne Ellis was unnaturally pale and that a group of boys were surrounding George Fenwick who had turned away to hide his tears. I overheard one boy say 'It's a shame, George. Everyone knows you're better than me and I've passed and you haven't.'

Felt disturbed.

Ah yes – 'the unnaturally pale girl!' Any supporter of segregation at eleven, whose heart has not wizened to a walnut, needs to see the 'unnaturally pale girl' only once to shatter his defence of it.

LOG BOOK

Of the three boys and three girls on the 11 Plus Borderline who went for interviews at the Melchester Grammar and High Schools respectively, two boys succeeded in obtaining places but all three girls were rejected.

JOURNAL

In the staff-room overheard Mrs. Grindle-Jones boasting that

12

the Mount Pleasant Prep. School (which her two children attended) had 'their usual success' in the Eleven Plus. It appears that 2 boys and 4 girls went from Mount Pleasant for Borderline interviews and one boy was offered a place by the Grammar School and all 4 girls got into the High School. It is maddening that all our girls were rejected whilst all theirs were accepted.

I asked the children what had happened at the Borderline and it appears that they first read a passage to Mr. Muttler (who owns Tampling Thread Factory and is Chairman of the Grammar/High Governors). Then the boys went to the Grammar School Headmaster who, amongst other things, asked each boy the number of ways a batsman could be 'outed' (although he is a Yorkshireman, they all agreed he said 'outed'), and who was their favourite film-star. The girls who went to the High School Headmistress were only asked by Miss Layer-Marney what their fathers did for a living and whereabouts in Tampling they lived.

HARPOLE TO MELCHESTERSHIRE DIRECTOR OF EDUCATION

Would it be possible for you to inform me of the criteria or marking system used in the Borderline interviews please? I am asking this because I note a curious discrepancy, this being that during the last three years only 8% of our girls sent for interview have been accepted at the Girls High School whereas 60% of the boys secured places at the Boys Grammar School.

TUSKER TO HARPOLE

I understand from Shire House that you have written demanding confidential information. All letters from schools must initially be addressed to my office and the decision whether or not to direct them elsewhere will be at my discretion. I consider your action a flagrant disregard of my authority.

CHIEF EDUCATION DIRECTOR TO HARPOLE

The information for which you ask is confidential. However, let me assure you that any variance in the numbers of places offered by the Melchester Grammar and High Schools is purely coincidental.

JOURNAL

Discreet inquiry elicited that in the last three years 15 girls from the Mount Pleasant Prep. School have been Borderline-interviewed for the Girls High School and all 15 were accepted. This disparity of 92% between the Prep. and our children puts beyond reasonable doubt my belief that undue social prejudice is shown.

HARPOLE TO J. R. MACDONALD DACRE, SOCIALIST COUNTY ALDERMAN FOR TAMPLING SOUTH WARD

I trust you will share my disturbance when I tell you that, during the last three years, only 8% of our Borderline girls have been offered High School places whereas 100% of the Prep. School girls secured them.

In fairness to the parents and children in your Ward do you not consider that this situation calls for investigation? I should be obliged if you would consider this communication *Very Confidential.*

DACRE TO HARPOLE

I have been told by Shire House that you have asked about this already. As you have carried out incorrect procedure you cannot expect me to interfere as it is now sub-judice. Furthermore I have never heard any complaints from anybody before about it, they not having come to my ears.

HARPOLE TO DACRE

If no-one has complained it is because no-one else has noticed this discrepancy. In any case, the parents of most of the children at this school are not big letter-writers. Thus, they must rely on

14

their *representative* to watch their interests. I should have thought the facts I have brought to your attention would have caused you to investigate what may be a flagrant exercise of social discrimination.

Please treat this as *VERY CONFIDENTIAL.*

There appears to be no answer to this letter.

JOURNAL

Happened to overhear Mrs. G-J. mention that her children attended Mount Pleasant at the same time as Alderman Dacre's daughter . . .

TUSKER TO HARPOLE

It has been brought to my notice that you have communicated with a County Alderman on educational business concerning your school. This is seriously out-of-order and both the Director of Education and I take a most serious view of this. Must it be necessary to tell you yet again that there are lines of communication laid down and these must be strictly adhered to and, in no circumstances, deviated from?

I may add that both the Director of Education and myself are reluctant to believe what others *may* – that you are insinuating unfairness in the Borderline Selection Procedure.

JOURNAL

Happened to meet Shutlanger, the Grammar School Head-master, in The Fusilier and, apropos of nothing, mentioned Alderman Dacre. 'That idle b*****d!' he exclaimed. 'He is no more a socialist than my ***e. It just suited him to say he was one to get a Union Secretary's job where he can sit on his ***e all day and get time off from doing Nothing to be a J.P., a Grammar/High School Governor, on the Hospital Board and any other top job he can hog combining minimum brains with

15

maximum puff. His Dad was a railway platelayer in the Glorious Dawn of 1924 and named him James Ramsay Macdonald Dacre and nobody yet has penetrated this disguise!'

One is torn between admiration for Harpole's quixotic foray into such hostile territory on an errand which, even if successful, can do him nothing but personal harm, and astonishment at his ingenuous belief that it is possible to wring damaging information from local government officials.

He might as well learn early as late the impossibility of defeating entrenched officials and the hopelessness of enlisting help from elected representatives (who have to scratch the backs of the same officials to obtain even a new sneck for some constituent's council-house door).

HARPOLE TO HIS FIANCEE, EDITH WARDLE

To-day there was a great commotion downstairs and it was Mrs. Teale screaming that the gas hot-water geyser would not stop. I did not consider this serious as it works on small coins and so would eventually stop from lack of them. However, when she began to call me *by name* I ran down and tore open the bathroom door whereupon Mrs. Teale appeared in a cloud of steam (which was as well).

'Stop it Mr. Harpole,' the silly creature kept screeching, 'Stop it before it blows my house up!'

I immediately rushed upstairs and obtained my moveable-spanner (a very expensive one Dad gave me last Christmas) and, shielding myself from the jet of steam issuing from the geyser, climbed on top of the bath (one foot on each side). But, before I had time to twist anything, the thing made a whining gasp and stopped! I shouted to Mrs. Teale to call in a plumber and she screamed back that she would and that it was all right to come out now as she was respectable again . . .

THEAKER TO HARPOLE (left on desk)

That Mrs. Foxberrow is messing up the furniture being the door and doorpost used for pulling out nibs.   (unsigned)

Visited Miss Foxberrow's classroom to give her the patent pen-nib extractor left behind for demonstration by a publisher's representative. There were loud noises emanating and on entering I found numerous children creeping on the floor between the desks making mooing sounds. I bent over one of these and asked, 'What are you doing, my dear?'

'I am demonstrating a cow grazing in its pasture,' she replied, and it was Miss Foxberrow with hair all over her face so all I could see was one eye as it were a forest animal peering from the undergrowth. I informed her that it was not my custom to call staff-ladies 'my dear'.

'Oh,' she said. 'Do you only call staff-*gentlemen* that?'

'What are you doing down there?' I asked, ignoring the implication.

'We are making a picture of Our Friend the Cow,' she answered, 'and, as is well known in *progressive* educational circles, unless a teacher can establish rapport between artist and subject, the resultant picture will be stale and, unless shown by an R.A., unprofitable.'

'Well, if that is so,' I said, 'why is Titus Fawcett painting his cow this bright vermilion red?'

'Oh well,' she said, 'if this is to be a Grand Palaver, I'll get up.' Which she did, putting on an artificial sigh. Then she picked up Fawcett's Red Cow and said, 'Children, Mr. Harpole does not like our exciting pictures. Perhaps he will tell us why, as we are all here to pick up any crumbs of learning that drop around.'

I was so exasperated by her flippancy that I told her sharply that she was to come with me into the corridor. 'I hope you are not going to do anything *ungentlemanly*, Mr. Harpole,' she said following me. I ignored this and, holding up the picture, said 'Now, if you want to know, it is not the colour but *them* I object to,' indicating the udders hanging from the animal and even scraping the ground. 'They are frankly indecent.'

'Well,' she said, 'if that is all that is bothering you, I will get Titus to paint on a skirt.' Since she still refused to regard the matter in a serious light, I told her that this permissiveness would give girls like Henrietta Billitt *ideas*. 'Rubbish!' she said. 'Living as she does in what is nothing more than a rural slum, the eight of them in two bedrooms and the privy down the garden,

17

she knows more about anatomy than the two of us put together. Since you have brought it up, when we painted "Our Mother and Father", Titus did his without a stitch on either and told me that, if I'd wanted them otherwise, I should have asked him to paint "Our Mother and Father with their Clothes on." '

So I told her that I hoped she would choose more conventional subjects such as Elves, Space Rockets and suchlike. Then, when I proffered her the patent pen-nib extractor, she replied airily, 'Oh, so Theaker has been sneaking has he? Well you can tell him we don't need his doorpost any more because, since I read a piece in last week's *Times Ed.*, we don't use pens; they cripple young children's conceptual flow. And, as for Theaker, surely one of the multiplying band of refugees from teaching, living on research grants, must have tumbled on the anthropological possibilities of caretakers? You should tip off Institutes of Education about his hiding-place.'

As I walked away she called, 'Are you quite fit again? Remember? You fell off your bike with that suitcase . . .'

For a young, inexperienced teacher she does not suffer from a deficiency of self-confidence. She is a disturbing influence in our school.

EMMA FOXBERROW TO FELICITY FOXBERROW

Darling Felix,
Absolutely numb with weariness and plastered to the neck in paste and things so but a line. No, shan't be home for the hunt do. Week-ends I flop. Face up to the bloodthirsty band as best you can. Screaming won't save you – use your knee.

The boss-man here is out of this world. He keeps taking a small clock hanging on a silver chain (with a large medal hanging to it) out of his waistcoat pocket and ostentatiously examining first *it* and then *me*. Yesterday I was whipping my kids into a frame of mind for child-masterpieces when in he marches looking like the End of the World and yelling, '*Where* is your teacher? Quiet! *Where* is your teacher?' Then he tore me off a strip or began to, but it ended up with him lamely asking me if I would mind not crawling about the floor, not that he minded but there was the Education Office and the Managers . . .

Ask Mummy to send me that tiger skin from one of the attics – I need it for Daniel in the Lion's Den.

18

Whilst checking the staff's weekly forecast of lessons I noted that Miss Foxberrow plans to give a painting lesson on Our Friend the Bull. This is so childishly meant for my provocation that I shall ignore it.

How pitiably inadequate is Harpole's equipment for rash expeditions upon such enchanted ground as What is or What is not a Good Picture! The ancient respectable yardstick of 'Your pictorial representation of that cow is what I also believe a cow to look like' *is utterly discredited nowadays by the cult worshippers of Child Art. How can it be that, despite the new universal education purveyed by Sunday Colour Supplements, Harpole does not yet know this? Picasso, like Kilroy, has been, and now three eyes are O.K.*

Councillor Mrs. Blossom visited the school and expressed a desire to see each class. When we came out of Mrs. Grindle-Jones's class, she took me aside and said it would be nice if the children stood up when she entered a room and called out, 'Good afternoon, Councillor Blossom.'

Feeling it incumbent upon myself to carry out her wishes, I preceded her into Miss Foxberrow's room but was disconcerted to find her receive my suggestion as though I was a half-wit.

Mrs. Blossom must have suspected this because, far from being mollified by the ragged cries of welcome, she insisted on checking the register. Most unfortunately she found that 45 children were recorded as being present whereas there were only 44 in attendance. Mrs. Blossom then crossed out the 45 and inserted 44 in red ink, initialled this and asked me to note it in the Log Book.

When we reached Room 4, Miss Tollemache greeted her with 'Oh, hello Annie,' and insisted on telling me that they had been in the same class at school and that their birthdays were within one week of each other. This information put Councillor Blossom into a huff and, when we were back in the corridor, she said, 'She may have attended the same school but I cannot remember her; from her appearance she must have left at least fifteen years before I arrived. Perhaps it was my mother she was thinking about . . .'

HARPOLE TO EDITH WARDLE

My chain came off twice on my way home so decided to adjust the back wheel of my bike. When I couldn't find my moveable-spanner in the place where I usually keep it, I worked out that I'd left it on the top of Mrs. Teale's gas-geyser the day it wouldn't stop. As it wasn't there either I decided the plumber who mended the geyser must have come across it and put it in with his own tools by mistake. But when I telephoned him, he said that there wasn't any need for him to even look in his tool-bag because there 'definitely had been no spanner on top of the geyser and what was I hinting at?' Well, I knew very well where I'd left it and, on top of that, I detected a note of triumph in his voice over the phone. You may not know it but my moveable-spanner was given me by Dad only a couple of Christmases ago and I well remember him saying that it was one of the two most useful tools a man could have. So you can understand why I am mad about losing it, dearest . . .

4

I should be greatly obliged if each member of the Staff would
take responsibility for conducting at least one morning service
this term and I suggest these dates:

May 12th	Mr. Croser
May 26th	Mrs. Grindle-Jones
June 9th	Mr. Pintle
June 23rd	Miss Foxberrow
July 7th	Miss Tollemache

*This is an interesting and encouraging innovation. Harpole must
know that it is a rare head teacher who can survive constant
erosion of his popularity by day-in day-out pontifical appearances
before teachers and children at 9.15 p.m. when both are at their
spiritual nadir. By exposing other teachers to the legal compulsion
of interceding daily with the Almighty, Harpole may well ensure
grudging sympathy towards his own inadequate petitions.*

JOURNAL

To-day, as I still have not been able to raise the down-payment
on the Ford I have set my heart on, I took our school football
team by public transport for their re-arranged last match of the
season with North End Primary Mixed. Oddly enough, Fred
Judd and Mrs. Trott, both on the local N.U.T. Committee, who
were travelling home from school on the same bus, pretended
not to see me. Later on in the evening I had a rum with
Shutlanger, the Grammar Head (who, incidentally, spends every
evening in The Fusilier since his wife ran off with a big lad

in his Sixth Form), and asked his opinion whether or not I was diminishing our Professional Image by escorting children on buses to out-of-school activities.

I find him difficult to follow when alcohol has gone to his head because his Oxford veneer slips and he relapses into the dialect he used as a boy. But he appeared to say, 'Sithee, surry, can t'see t'doctor tekking his b****y panel-patients to hospital on a double-decker bus?'

This seemingly was his final word on the subject because he began to tell me repetitiously how he had lost seven pounds on a horse. ('It was *****y pulled,' he kept muttering.)

I reflected that Mr. Chadband never took boys on buses to matches nor did he ever even ask if we had won or lost. Yet he was highly regarded up at the Office and has often told me how he was made a Head (with a school-house to be married into) before he was twenty-seven. In future, I intend to disregard Croser's excuse that he only knows the rules of Rugby League football and shall insist that he escorts the lads to away fixtures where I shall meet them on arrival.

Of course Harpole is not damaging whatever image he imagines the public venerates. In fact, surrounded by small boys dangling their football kit like trophies of war and vaingloriously prophesying in shrill voices how many goals they personally mean to score, he is presenting the best possible front to the travelling ratepayers – a public employee with his sleeves rolled up and on the job.

By using his own time – and since he works in a primary school it is his own time he will have to use – Harpole is doing more for professional esteem than all the hot air being blown out of every union meeting within twenty-five miles of his bus route.

But drinking rum of an evening! However, it may be that his mention of this bizarre activity is only meant to convince himself that he has an unconventional, even eccentric side to his humdrum nature.

JOURNAL

Councillor Mrs. Blossom visited the school to enquire if all was well.

She told me that she was confident that I would succeed and that it was no secret that she hoped Mr. Chadband would retire so that '*we all*' could have the benefit of some young blood. Old men like him and Mr. Blossom are nothing but a hindrance and encumbrance to us 'young ones'.

She then asked me if I did not agree that Free Meals and Family Allowances should be stopped. 'Britain is a land of layabouts', she said. 'If I had my way I would have some of them doctored like tomcats, living like lords as they do on National Assistance. But I am sure you share my views.' I readily agreed. However, after she had gone, I felt uneasy because my views actually are not the same as Councillor Blossom's.

This morning Mrs. Grindle-Jones drew my attention to her free-standing blackboard, complaining not without cause that, at her age, she should not be expected to erect it as her doctor had warned her that there were a lot of slipped discs about at this time of the year. She added that Mr. Grindle-Jones had advised her that, should she injure herself whilst erecting the board, she would be justified in asking the Office for industrial compensation. On examination, I found the structure to be unlike any other known to me as it consists of two boards of black wood riveted to each side of an immense steel plate, making three boards in all. In addition, there is a small cast-iron escutcheon: WHITEHOUSE, TIPTON, STAFFS
NEW PATENT BLACKBOARD 1853
I tested the weight and it is indeed of extreme weight. I promised to write in to the Office requesting the installation of the new roller-type with which she said Mr. Grindle-Jones's school is fited out from end to end.

TUSKER TO HARPOLE

I am astonished to receive your request for a new blackboard. May I draw your attention to:

(*a*) The last date for requisition of permanent equipment and teaching aids for installation during the next financial year was February 28th last.

(*b*) I note that you state the equipment you describe is *heavy*, not *unserviceable*. It is not County policy to replace equipment which is still serviceable.

I showed Mr. Tusker's letter to Mrs. Grindle-Jones and asked her to soldier on for eighteen months when I felt confident that a new roller-board would be the reward of her patience and understanding. She did not respond favourably to this.

MR. GRINDLE-JONES TO HARPOLE

Strictly confidential

My wife tells me of your dilemma. I should not wish to be quoted but her misfortune is the direct result of poor Chadband's not keeping up with the times. However, I do not wish my wife's health to be impaired by the daily erection of a prehistoric monument and I happen to know that several free-standing blackboards, which were superannuated from my school here at Sinderby-le-Marsh many years ago, presently are stored in an outhouse behind the Education Office. I suggest you request the lightest of these.

HARPOLE TO TUSKER

I regret failing to note that the correct date for requesting permanent equipment had passed and am sorry to have inconvenienced you.

As I understand that there are a number of old and unwanted blackboards in an outhouse behind your administrative offices, I wonder if I might be allowed to exchange my overweight board? If you will permit this, I will arrange for Mr. Theaker to collect it.

THEAKER TO HARPOLE (note left on desk)

About that taking and fetching the union says to inform you it is not my job and to only go under protest. He says for you to sign a paper promising compensation for any accident to my person contracted on the journey to and fro as I am not covered by the Offices.

Cycled to the Offices and as Mr. Tusker was not in, asked Mr. Minchin, the Clerk, if he would show me the redundant blackboards. To my annoyance he refused, adding gratuitously that schools seemed to think that the Office had nothing else to do except to run about on their behalf and that he knew *nothing* of 'this blackboard business' and would do *nothing* without Mr. Tusker's authorization. 'Well,' I said, 'at least lend me the key so that I can examine if there is anything suitable.' When he refused this small favour also, I asked him to please forget the matter and not to mention my visit to Mr. Tusker. Felt humiliated and depressed.

TUSKER TO HARPOLE

My Clerk informs me that you have demanded access to his equipment store which he rightly refused.

Please note that I do not tolerate interference with my administration staff by head-teachers. Note also that future requests of this nature must be put in writing and addressed to me through the usual channels.

JOURNAL

Met Shutlanger, far gone, in The Fusilier last night and told him about the blackboard. 'Oh those little runts (meaning Mr. Tusker and Mr. Minchin), I have had Big Trouble with them in my time. But I am on their wavelength now and they know it.' He then scribbled for a few minutes on the back of a cancelled betting slip and said, 'Sithee, copy this out just as it is and send it to t'silly buggers and watch what happens.' He then told me he had won eleven pounds on a horse called Pretty Polly. Since I saw him last he has made considerable progress with a Tariq Ali moustache.

HARPOLE TO TUSKER

I wish to report the following accident. Whilst erecting an unusually heavy blackboard yesterday I twisted my back. The resultant injury at present is not sufficient to prevent my attendance at school, but I am advised by my Union solicitor that such injuries occasionally result in partial or permanent disability and that I should request that the circumstances of the accident be officially recorded by my employers on the appropriate Ministry of Insurance form should it become necessary at some future date to claim compensation from them. I have made an appropriately dated entry in the Official School Log.

JOURNAL

To my astonishment Mr. Tusker arrived at 9.15 a.m. and asked to inspect the iron-bound blackboard. Visibly straining, he lifted it, exclaiming breathlessly, 'I cannot understand what all the to-do is about: it seems no more than a normal weight to me.'

'Well, Mr. Tusker,' I said jocularly, 'then keep your feet where they are and release it.'

He did not respond in similar vein to this but gingerly lowered the board and inexpertly leaned it against the easel. This, being unable to withstand the great weight, immediately snapped-to and collapsed, bringing down a vase of Sweet-Williams and scattering a box of chalk-pieces, Mr. Tusker leaping away with surprising nimbleness.

'Since you insist,' he said grudgingly, 'this board may be changed with one of the redundant ones in my outhouse. Make a note of it in the Official Log. And I fail to see why it has been necessary to make a fuss about so trivial a matter or why I should be bothered with details of this nature. The title "Post of Responsibility" these days seems to have no meaning except as entitlement to extra, unearned salary.'

Tusker indeed must have been severely shaken by his escape from injury to have passed so frank an opinion of Posts of Responsibility (often renamed 'Graded Posts' by incumbents sensitive to their lack of responsibility). Right as he is, the blame for this grandiose title being more honoured in breach than in observance belongs to the many heads who battle on from ulcer to ulcer determinedly clinging to each vestige of power until they falter away at 65 to die (often unrepentant) at some watering-place.

Tusker, of course, is right: he should never have heard of this

26

blackboard business. But, as the Peter Principle emphasizes, in all mature bureaucracies, executives eventually rise to their own Level of Incompetence. Thus Tusker justifies his avoidance of tackling the larger issues by grubbing around for petty business to fill in his time.

Mercifully, little pockets of competence always exist much further down the ladder. Harpole should have looked for the clerk tea-maker (often called Perce or Em), and he would have been fixed up with his blackboard and no-one the wiser.

JOURNAL

Had a telephone call from a person called Flora who said she was 'only the office dogsbody', but she had been 'told by a little bird' that I wanted a blackboard and she had put one out for me in the laurels behind the store shed, adding 'Saturday morning would be a good time to pick it up but not to say anything about it to "you know who".'

HARPOLE TO EDITH WARDLE

... and I am glad you are interested in my moveable-spanner and keep asking about it because, as it happens I was thinking about it only two nights ago when I couldn't sleep and I decided that the plumber has 'won' it. That is a war-time expression meaning to take a fancy to something and to move it to another place unknown to its owner but convenient to oneself. So, next evening, I went to the police station. Not wishing to be had for slander, I reported it as Lost Property.

The sergeant was most unhelpful and put on an aggrieved air.

'Ah well,' he said grudgingly, 'I suppose I shall have to write it all down. Where did you lose it?' When I told it was in my landlady's bathroom, he put on an act as if I was mad. 'Are you insinuating that your landlady stole it?' he asked even more truculently, to which I replied 'That is not for me to say. I have told you the salient facts and I expect your detectives to assist in its recovery.'

'Well I have written it all down,' he said, 'and now I have some work to do relating to *crime*. We will inform you *if* your tool is brought in.'

5

This morning Mr. Festing visited, complaining with unnecessary emphasis that Croser had taught his child, Martha, that the steeple of Chesterfield Church had a bend in it whereas, whilst on their way on the family holiday to Rhyl last summer and passing through Chesterfield, he personally had explained to Martha and her mother that it only *appeared* to be leaning, it being an optical illusion and, in reality, as straight as any other steeple, as had been proved by mathematics. He claimed that Croser had thus undermined his parental authority by causing Martha to doubt his wisdom.

'But it is well known that the steeple there is twisted,' I said. 'It is categorically stated to be twisted in Arthur Mee and, in fact, the townsfolk are proud of this distinguishing feature, pointing out to strangers its similarity to the Leaning Tower of Pisa. In fact, when there was a move made to pull it down and re-erect it, the shopkeepers did all in their power to obstruct this because it brought coach-trips from all over the Midlands, whilst other ratepayers wrote to the newspapers pointing out that they had found the fact an acceptable means of entering into conversation with strangers when on holiday.' (As do the people of Wigan with their pier.)

'This is all nonsense,' Mr. Festing interrupted angrily. 'I have studied it *scientifically* and it only *looks* crooked.' He then insisted that I compel Croser to retract his statement and explain that the steeple was really straight. When I demurred, he went off in a rage, threatening that he would go 'above my head' about it as it was a terrible thing when a father had his authority 'flouted by a set of damned official parasites who did nothing but live off the ratepayers . . .'

I found a way of mentioning this to young Croser apropos something else and told him that I had dealt with the matter.

However, he showed no hint of gratitude but exclaimed airily, 'Well, if he thinks Chesterfield steeple is straight, he ought to have his head examined. It is well known that he is a Domestic Tyrant and you only have to see his poor doormat of wife as proof of it. It is a wonder he does not picket travel agencies warning people not to go on cruises for fear they might sail off the edge of the Earth.'

Croser gets on my nerves.

HARPOLE TO EDITH WARDLE

. . . I found Shutlanger, the Grammar School Head, in The Fusilier, drinking to excess as per usual. Nevertheless, I asked him for an opinion on Festing's complaint. All I could get from him was, 'It all boils down to ******g sex. That's my last word on the *****y peep-show.' He then told me in a maudlin stage whisper that it was all around that Miss Cluff, who has been recently appointed Headmistress of Childe Monkspath village school (with house attached) had only got the job because she was Mr. Tusker's 'concubine' and that he honoured her every Friday between 3 and 3.45 p.m., having first granted the children Extra Play.

This is manifestly absurd as Miss Cluff is quite elderly and a Strict Baptist. It was obvious that he had heard (as everyone else in Tampling has) that the big sixth-former who went off with his wife has been given a place at the London School of Economics – where you would expect such disruptive elements as him to end up . . .

JOURNAL

Checking Miss Tollemache's Register of Attendance, I became aware of several serious errors in accounting. Lucinda Bull, who is in hospital, had been marked as Present all week, there was a discrepancy of 29 between the aggregate of half-daily attendances and the aggregate of individual attendances, and the weekly attendance summary was 17% inaccurate. To further confusion, numerous children had been marked as being Absent and Present at the same time.

29

I therefore spent a considerable time writing a detailed analysis of her mistakes going back to the beginning of term and inserted this in her register where she will be sure to find it when she next opens it. Some teachers do not appear to understand that a register is an Official Document.

EMMA FOXBERROW TO FELICITY FOXBERROW

No, I *won't* answer all your questions, Felix. Life is *not* passing you by. First, pass your A Levels and all things will be added unto you. And it is *not* true that I work in a madhouse. Most of the time, things slouch along very mildly. I only bother to recount the *bizarre*. Like yesterday.

Just before opening-time, I heard a wailing noise next door and found Miss Tollemache (fiftyish and of locally gentle birth) stood bhd her desk staring at her register and mkg an extraordinary keening sound, in monoplay. I pushed a chair under her but the lamentation abated not a whit. So I brt The Old School (Pintle) charging up. 'Ah,' he says, 'I've seen this coming on. It's her Time of Life.'

Well, G. Harpole comes steaming in and flaps around. 'Be still, Miss Tollemache, please be still!' he bleats, 'Please remember the children.'

Then Grindle-Jones puts her head round the door, lifts her grizzled eyebrows and calls loudly, 'Shall I ring the bell? It's five to nine.' Of course Let the Heavens fall, Routine is God to G. H. and he shouts wildly, 'Do! Do!'

Well, he then realizes that forty-odd big-eyed, big-eared witnesses are about to be admitted and dashes to Tollemache, picks up a piece of paper lying on her register, holds it before her face like smelling salts and then dramatically tears it in half. Magic! She shuts off steam and throttles down to a gentle sniffing.

'It's alright, Miss Tollemache,' he coos. 'Please don't be upset. You can keep doing it as you've always done it.'

All very mysterious! (To be cont'd . . .)

TUSKER TO HARPOLE

I have received a communication from a member of your staff,

Miss Grace Tollemache. This intimates that she is contemplating resignation because she feels that she cannot perform her duties to – I quote – 'the superhuman standard Mr. Harpole expects of us and this is causing me great distress.'

I would draw attention to:

(*a*) the high esteem in which the Primary School Managers hold Miss Tollemache's services over the last thirty years and that they are not unmindful of the distinguished public service of her father, County Alderman J. W. Tollemache.

(*b*) the impossibility of filling a vacancy should one arise.

In these circumstances I should be obliged if you would arrange an appointment with my Secretary so that I can have a detailed report on how this regrettable incident arose.

JOURNAL

Visited the Office and assured Mr. Tusker that I had withdrawn any suggestions which might cause Miss Tollemache emotional distress. Even so, he instructed me to make out a full and detailed written statement and demanded a copy of the note inserted in her register. Came away feeling low-spirited, his last words being that the Office was unlikely to recognize potential head-teacher-material in anyone who 'made a god of petty clerical mumbo-jumbo to frustrate dedicated teachers.'

I was very impressed by Mr. Tusker's desk top. The only papers on it were in the Out tray which was full and I compared it with my own desk top where new problems settle faster than I can clear off the old ones.

Harpole has been hard done by here. Granted that he would have done better to have had a quiet word with Miss Tollemache about her hazy arithmetic rather than ambushing her with a catalogue of her incompetence. He might even have found it less nervous strain to overlook her sketchy accountancy and to resign himself to a weekly exercise in forgery on her register.

If Miss Foxberrow's high-spirited account is to be believed, Pintle's off-the-cuff pronunciamento may well be right and Harpole would do well to leave her to her own ways so long as only registers suffer. Since these vexatious documents nowadays serve

31

only *marginal* use and are bound to disappear from the educational scene they have tyrannized too long, Harpole could rig them without fear of detection – particularly after Tusker has uncharacteristically described them as 'clerical mumbo-jumbo.' (*One supposes that Harpole will have been most careful to file this valuable letter . . .*)

And Tusker's clear desk must not cause him to repine. If problems are dumped at Harpole's door, it is only because others still trust in his goodwill and ability to solve them. Whereas Tusker plainly suffers from Papyrophobia* (*sufferers make a virtue of a clear desk whereas they really are suppressing reminders of the work they cannot do*). And the description of his Out file suggests that his Chief Clerk, Minchin, is a Fileomaniac (*total immersion in keeping files inconclusive but up-to-date*).

*See: *The Peter Principle.*

32

6

. . . as I was wending my way to the staff-room for playtime-tea, two little girls from Croser's class approached seeking my consent to a White Elephant sale, the proceeds to go to the Poor. I said Yes, that would be in order, but they pursued me down the corridor asking, 'When?' 'Where?' 'Could they go round the classrooms to ask for White Elephants?' 'Would I help them with the pricings?'

By the time I had made all the arrangements for them and given precise instructions (which I made them repeat as is my custom) the internal warning-bell had gone and then the brass bell brought the children streaming back into school. This was most aggravating because I wanted to tell the staff of our great victory over Melchester Goodge Road Primary who not only have twice our number to pick from but also have the Problem Family Rehabilitation Centre in their zone (which gives them a reservoir of players of unexampled ferocity.)

However, I suppose one must encourage initiative in a good cause in our children, but you can imagine my feelings when I found all the staff (except Mr. Pintle) still lolling about in easy chairs in a haze of cigarette smoke. I pointedly left the door ajar and waved aside the fug as I poured out my tea – no-one proffering to serve me as was always expected by Mr. Chadband.

'Oh Lord!' Mrs. G-J. said. 'Don't tell me – *they're* in again. Lord, how playtime flies!'

Last night I was invited to the monthly smoker of the Royal & Ancient Order of Buffaloes and obliged with 'Trade Winds', 'Sea Fever' and 'The Fighting Temeraire' which went down very well.

TEMPORARY NOTICE PLEASE CIRCULATE

I should be obliged if Staff would leave the Staff-room immediately on hearing the internal warning-bell which is sounded for that purpose. When the playground brass bell sounds, Staff should be awaiting their children at their doors so as to ensure orderly movement in the corridors and a quiet resumption of work.

Like Satan, Harpole has been bound in Chadband's ways for a thousand years. He ought to know that teachers conform only reluctantly to circulated admonition. He would have achieved his desirable exercise of getting his pickets into position just as well by breezing into the staff-room and saying lightly, ' Yea, the fields are white unto harvest but the labourers are few.' Or some equally fatuous extract from Holy Writ. And by issuing precise instructions on How to run a Sale, Harpole is educating the children for slavery. A school is not a factory. Its raison d'être is to provide opportunity for experience.

MRS. SUSAN BYRD TO HARPOLE

We are moving to Tampling in the near future and I wish to select a school for Elspeth aged nine. The L.E.A. has suggested three schools geographically convenient and I am writing separately to each.

I am a subscribing member of the Advisory Centre for Education and would be obliged if you would answer these queries:

(*a*) How old is your building?
(*b*) Are there internal lavatories with adjacent hand-washing facilities?
(*c*) What percentage of children in the appropriate age-group were selected for High School in the last three years?
(*d*) Is corporal punishment used?
(*e*) Have you a P.T.A.?

I feel sure that you will agree that making a choice of a good school for one's child is most important.

I expect you have had that confounded load of cheek from a
Mrs. Byrd ferreting into this and that. I have written telling her
that one school is as good as another, all being run by *experts*
and I know you will do the same.

Some of these modern parents are the limit forever interfering
and poking into what is none of their business. I don't know
what Tusker was up to even giving her our addresses. I shall
raise this at the next Headmasters' Association meeting.

JOURNAL

An unusual person called to-day. 'Hello!' she said brightly,
'I'm Sue Byrd.' She was wearing a red, black and orange jersey
well up her legs like a footballer and had two strings of baubles
dangling to her waist. She told me that a magazine for parents
called *WHERE?* had given her a list of schools so that she could
assess their suitability for her nine year old child, Elspeth.

'I'll be frank,' she said. 'When I saw your answers, the age of
your building, that you only had outside loos and occasionally
smacked the kids I more or less ruled you out. Then I thought –
in fairness – I at least ought to look in on their teaching.'

I explained that I felt this wouldn't give her a true impression
because a stranger in a classroom creates an artificial situation (a
useful phrase picked up on a refresher course).

'Oh,' she said, 'that's all right. I can tell all I want to know just
by *looking* at a person.'

I then told her firmly that qualified teachers, like doctors and
dentists and all professional people, did not consider it necessary
to be inspected by prospective clients.

'Those are not good analogies,' she said pertly. 'Barristers and
judges don't mind being watched, nor do butchers or black-
smiths. And any parent can *try* a doctor or a dentist before
letting them loose on one's children.'

I had never thought of it like that before and it now occurred
to me that this indeed was true. There are only very few jobs,
like engine-drivers, steeplejacks and town clerks, where circumstances deter close public examination. Nevertheless I

35

stuck to my guns and she went, saying her next call was to be on 'a Mr. Judd' who, she had been told, 'had a twentieth-century building'.

Just as I was going home, Pintle, almost incoherent, rage intermingled with grief, burst accusingly in. This being the season of the year when he does the Normans, he had been to the Surplus Apparatus and Staff Illustration Store to put back his Viking longship (made of 3,500 matchsticks) and to take out his cardboard Norman Keep. Apparently the Store was empty and the Keep (which he had made in his first year out of college) had gone. I hurried back with him and the little room was certainly empty of educational apparatus and now housed brushes, mops, cleaning paraphernalia, a child's desk and an old armchair.

As I gazed unbelievingly at this, Theaker came round the corner. He was taken aback but rallied, declaring defiantly before I had time to speak, 'Well, it was only full of junk.'

'Junk!' exclaimed Pintle, for once almost bereft of speech.

'What is this desk doing here?' I demanded, going straight to what I perceived was the nub of things.

'It is for my paper-work.'

'But you have no clerical work.'

'Since I have had this desk I have,' he replied with some self-satisfaction.

He then handed me a sheaf of paper comprising a list of teachers' names and addresses, the average numbers of milk bottles delivered during the previous year, the number of chairs and desks and blackboards in each room and so on. 'I am just beginning to write out the names of all the children,' he said.

'But nobody needs this information,' I said hotly. 'And, if they did, I already have it.'

'Somebody might want to know it when you are off on your long holidays,' he countered.

I noticed that he had written on one sheet – 'Moved a desk from Room 3 to Room 4.'

'Who wants to know *that*?' I demanded. 'You spent as long writing it as doing it.'

'It confirms I did it,' he said stubbornly. 'Now that it's on paper . . .'

'But I can *see* for myself you've done it,' I said, exasperated. 'We are not in the Foreign Legion sending signals from one desert fort to another.'

36

('What have you done with my Norman Keep?' moaned Pintle.)

Unable to grasp this innuendo, Theaker went on, 'And I shall be wanting an assistant now.'

'Now *what*? I cried. 'Now that you have a desk? You don't need an assistant. You can manage your job adequately on your own.'

'Not with all this paper work to get through,' he said.

Realizing that I was losing face before Pintle, I controlled myself and said in calm but firm tones, 'Mr. Theaker, this room must be emptied before nine in the morning and everything that was in it put back.' Then, to prevent further argument, I turned sharply on my heel, leaving Pintle to wrest back his own fortress.

Harpole's indignation is excessive. Theaker is merely practising a very mild exercise in Peter's well-known principle – In a Hierarchy Every Employee Tends to Rise to His Level of Incompetence. *Indeed, this is an integral pillar in the educational structure. Tusker, himself, once perhaps a first-rate physics master, by struggling upwards to his Level of Incompetence is now a well-to-do fifth-rate administrator.*

HARPOLE TO EDITH WARDLE

... A fortnight having gone by and no intimation from Mrs. Teale that the detectives had visited about my moveable-spanner, I felt indignant and visited the Police Station. The Sergeant greeted me as if he had never seen me before. 'What can we do for *you*?' he asked coldly. When I reminded him of my loss he said airily, 'Oh, that trifling matter! Nobody has handed it in yet.'

I went away feeling frustrated since he knew he had got the better of me and was rubbing it in. I should have said sarcastically, 'Well you don't expect it to come walking in and give itself up, do you?'

7

As a modest innovation I would like all classes to arrange an Outside-Visit to stimulate the interests of the children in the World-Around-Us. Afterwards, a project could stem from this, little booklets made, models constructed and so on.

Note that this is approved by the most modern educational thought. Please let me know the Centre-of-Interest you propose to visit.

RETURNED CIRCULAR

The Backwards – Miss Tollemache		The Alderman Tollemache Old Folks' Home.
Class 1	– Mr. Croser	Woburn Abbey
Class 2	– Mr. J. A. Pintle	Messrs. Muttler & Son's Thread Factory
Class 3	– Mrs. Rita Grindle-Jones	Barchester Cathedral
Class 4	– Emma Foxberrow	The Confluence of the Elver and the Alder

EXTRACTS FROM WEEKLY FORECASTS AND RECORD BOOKS

Miss Tollemache	Aim of educational visit – to foster civic pride
Mr. Croser	Aim – to study how the Rich live and Evolution at the zoo there

Mr. Pintle	Aim – to prepare class for work in future life.
Mrs. Grindle-Jones	Aim – to teach the children the glory of God as manifested by man's handiwork here below.
Emma Foxberrow	Aim – to have an exciting time (see Paulerbury's *Education for a Free Society*, pp. 137-9).

FREE WRITING BY EUNICE COWPER (Class 3)

On Friday our teacher Mrs. Grindle-Jones escorted us on our longed-for excursion to Barchester Cathedral. On our way there on the coach some boys at the back began to sing but our teacher forbade them reminding them that we were not going to a football match but to the house of God. It was very beautiful in the ediface. Some boys asked if they could climb up to the tower and our teacher said that they could not. Some boys asked if they could go down to the crip and our teacher said they could not. A clergyman in a long robe showed us the beautiful tomb of the famous Bishop who led the army which defeated the Scots in 1294 with great slaughter. We were also showed the beautiful memorial to Lord de la Saville who defeated the Lancastrians in 1432 with great slaughter. We were then taken to a beautiful vestry where another gentleman who was called the Reverend C.P.R. Smith gave us a long and excellent talk on the history of everything. Then we came home. This time the boys did not try to sing.

EMMA FOXBERROW TO FELICITY FOXBERROW

Thank you darling for the wellington received safely by parcel post. No, I am not going round the bend. I only needed *one* because I have only lost *one*. But now I am made whole I can go back and look for the one I lost! I lost it on the Great Educational Expedition ordained by G. Harpole. I traipsed off with my lot to find the confluence of the mighty streams that water this land before forming the Atlantic Ocean, to wit the Elver and the Alder, mainly because, except for the Ordnance Survey work-gangs, no-one ever *does* see where rivers meet up and partly because, on so short a journey, no-one could possibly be sick. The kids were not to keen, especially as they knew Croser was taking his lot to the zoo and amusement park at Woburn, but they cheered up when I said they could write a message and seal it in a bottle. I promised that I would give the tiger's head Mummy sent as a prize to the one who had a message returned from the furthest place, say Fiji or Japan.

The first hitch came predictably from a herd of bullocks. 'Predictably' because it is well known in educational circles that bullocks always ambush school parties venturing off main roads. Enough to say that I lost my wellington on the field of battle.

The Confluence was a let-down – two muddy ditches reluctantly co-operating to produce a slightly wider muddy ditch. So I injected some romance into the proceedings by bidding each child advance in turn, bow to the River God and, before throwing in the bottled letter, to cry, 'O Great Spirit of the Elver & Alder, hear my cry and bear my Message far upon the bosom of thy Tide.' Honestly you never saw such a collection. It was the social history of Tampling South Ward – scent bottles, pop bottles, National Health bottles (a lot of these) and beer bottles. And they didn't shift. They just oozed turgidly around. I'd never quite realized what a mob 45 kids are until I saw this armada becalmed . . .

FREE WRITING BY TITUS FAWCETT

. . . the best was when we were attacked by some big cows they were jigantic like in Daktary. All the children ran screaming and I did as well. But Miss Foxberrow stood firm and drew her umbrella and *I* shouted Boys, Miss Foxberrow will be gored to death like in a bullfight and most of them came back especially Henrietta Billitt and we regrouped around our leader. Then Miss Foxburrow raised her umbrella and cried Charge! and we counter-attacked like the U.S. Cavalry in Wagon Train. And Henrietta Billitt charged by my side and the cows turned tail and fled and while we were pursuing them through a bog Miss Foxberrow lost a boot and couldn't find it. The rest of the way back she hopped and I helped her and Miss Foxberrow praised our bravery and said she would remember it to her dying day and that this was the biggest adventure she had ever had.

MRS. TED JENKINSON TO HENRIETTA BILLITT

Dear Henrietta my husband come across your bottle down by
the sluice at burlap Common and I am writing to you I have five
children of my own and hope you win your teachers prize and I
wonder what it will be I also have thirteen grandchildren my
husband Ted and me wishes you all the best we are doing the
sitting room so I will go now.

Bye bye and oblige

MISS CELIA LONGBOTTOM TO TITUS FAWCETT

I found your bottle down by Burlap Common sluice gate where
there was a lot of bottles stuck in the mud and when I was
reading it my boy friend said it was a trick to have people on
and snatched it and threw it back into the water. But I remembered your name and address and I am writing to you to claim
this Reward. I think you have a nice name and your writing is
very neat my boy friend is called Ed and he is not a good scholar
and was in the C's but he doesn't know I know that. I was a good
scholar at school but I didn't pass for the high school so I work
in the thread factory and unless you have to don't do the same
as it is dull and they don't pay much. We are going to be married
next Easter.
p.s. My age is almost 18 and I have short red hair gray eyes and
I walk with a limp due to having an accident falling off Eds
B.S.A. when he was working up to a ton. S.W.A.L.K.

TUSKER TO HARPOLE

I enclose a communication from The Clerk to the Elver &
Alder Catchment Board. Kindly report complete details of this
deplorable occurrence and note that it must not recur.
*1 enclosure
   'My attention has been drawn to the fact that, set afloat by
one of your schools, numerous glass receptacles have been
located by my staff travelling seawards on a waterway of
this Authority. May I point out with justification the
irresponsibility of this regrettable occurrence and suggest

that you draw the attention of the teacher responsible to
Section 9 of the Elver & Alder Catchment Board's Bye-
Laws 1947 and that anyone convicted of an offence as listed
may be liable to a fine not exceeding £25.'

JOURNAL

Decide not to show Tusker's and the River Clerks' letters to
Miss Foxberrow for fear that they might discourage her
initiative, which I am beginning to admire. In a roundabout
manner, discovered the facts from a child, Henrietta Billitt,
and sent them to the Office, adding that Miss Foxberrow is young
and inexperienced, her fault only being over-enthusiasm. But I
resented having to write such a letter. Sometimes I wonder if
promotion is worth all this lick-spittle.

Croser having predictably put off booking a coach to Woburn
until it was too late to secure one, substituted a journey on a
Service bus to Nun Leeming where there is a derelict church in
the middle of the fields.

COVERING NOTE TO PARCEL FROM TITUS FAWCETT
TO EMMA FOXBERROW AT HER ROOMS

Dear Madam,
My Dad took Henrietta Billitt and me to the Confluence as he
was very interested in my description of what we did. He also
took a bottle with a Message in and threw it in. He did not say
what the Message was but said he wasn't going to be as stupid
as us and put his address inside so that some jack-in-office
could persecute him. Then my Dad found your boot because he
said his eyes are the sharper through not wearing them out
reading. It was Henrietta Billitt who cleaned and polished up
the boot.

JOURNAL

Croser, looking less complacent than his usual self, asked to see
me at 4 p.m. He had with him a child, Vincent Slope, and an

untidy parcel made out of the *Daily Mirror* from which, to my astonishment, he removed a skull, mahogany in colour and obviously very antique. Having laid this in my In-tray he reported that Slope had proudly brought this for his class Interest Table the day after the history trip. The child who had been looking apprehensive then burst into tears and, before I had time to demand from where he had obtained the skull, sobbed that he had found it adjacent to the ruined church at Nun Leeming. On being pressed by me he agreed that he had 'scratched it up' from below the chancel floor.

'But was it not fastened to anything else?' I demanded. He did not appear to understand what I meant by this so I asked, 'Where is the rest of *it*?' Until then, the child did not fully understand the gravity of his action and he sobbed that 'the head was all there was in the hole.'

'What Mr. Harpole is saying,' Croser interrupted, 'is that you are guilty of Desecration.'

'A child of nine cannot possibly understand the meaning of the word,' I said coldly.

'Mr. Harpole means that you have done an Awful Thing, you wicked boy,' Croser said without turning a hair at my rebuff. 'He means that you have annoyed God who will punish you.'

I ignored this ridiculous interpretation of Sin and told the child to wait outside and then told Croser in no uncertain terms that he must take the boy back and see that the skull was re-buried in consecrated ground as close to the rest of the deceased as could be determined. When he protested that it was miles off and nowhere near a bus service and then at least a good mile's 'footslog' from a road, I firmly pointed out that a Diocesan Faculty had to be obtained before an exhumation and the consequences to him should it all come out in the *Sentinel*. He then went off in a huff.

I thought it unwise to record this in the Log.

JOURNAL

Croser, looking his usual self-satisfied self, told me that he had gone to the Slope's house 'as per *your instructions*' and had been told by Mrs. Slope that I had no jurisdiction over Vincent after 4 p.m. and he was not to go back to the 'spooky place' and that, anyway, her husband had dug a hole at the bottom of his allotment and 'the head was in it and there it would stay.' Felt disturbed not knowing what the outcome will be if this becomes public knowledge as people are irrational about the departed.

OFFICIAL LOG BOOK

Mr. Croser, Certificated Assistant, reported giving permission to one child to punch another. He has expressed regret for this unfortunate episode.

HARPOLE TO EDITH WARDLE

Croser in a pitiful funk told me that, when Martha Festing told him that Vincent Slope had pinched her whilst they were marching from Morning Service, he had ordered Slope to remain stationary whilst the girl retaliated. He swore it had nothing to do with the skull and almost grovelled. 'Will they make me resign over it?' he kept saying. 'Or will his Dad have me "summonsed"?' Gave him short shrift saying he'd be lucky if *both* didn't happen and, for such utter stupidity, he deserved whatever he got and I didn't feel that I could support him. Really it baffles me! And yet normally this same Croser is a monument of self-approbation . . .

EMMA FOXBERROW TO FELICITY FOXBERROW

. . . And for once the odious Croser is discomfited. He has a monster called Vincent Slope in his class, an only child indulged by his parents and who has been a thorn in the side of every teacher who has had him. They say he was smacked once (in the Infants) and his parents came up and made such a fuss, threatening prosecution and what-not, that no-one tht it worthwhile tackling him agn and just prayed for the day he could be legitimately passed on to the next sufferer at the year-end, contenting themselves with filling his Record Card with a catalogue of lawlessness. He is a miserably thin youth with protruding eyes and a vicious mouth. It is horrifying that some day an unfortunate woman and chn will have this unspeakable bully for a husband and father. They wd be better off as Barbary slaves.

Well, the cowardly Croser let him get away with murder too, but on Tuesday he must have been still raw from a tremendous rocket G. Harpole gave him over this same Slope and a skull, because when Martha Festing, a nice little girl, protested tha Slope had cruelly pinched her, Croser rose to glory and ordered two boys to hold the little bully's arms and commanded little Martha to exact justice, which she did with a surprisingly violent straight-left to the nose. There was much heartless laughter and Monster burst into tears and his nose into blood.

Croser now slinks abt like a condemned criminal

OFFICIAL LOG BOOK

Mr. V. Slope visited the school and made allegations that his son has been mistreated by Mr. Croser, one of the assistant teachers. I expressed my regret and promised to investigate the complaint.

JOURNAL

Slope (senior) slid into my room this afternoon, a pale cunning looking man with three ball-point pens in his breast pocket and an R.A.F. tie. He began by saying he had been disturbed for some time by reports going around the district of the weak discipline since Mr. Chadband, 'for whom he had the greatest admiration', had left, that all the neighbours were talking about it and there was some talk of getting up a petition 'to the Authorities' but he personally had decided to give me the benefit of the doubt until yesterday . . .

I contained my rising fury by noting that Mr. Chadband had written on his unspeakable child's Record Card:

Mr. Slope is a trouble maker and cunning about it. He invariably begins by saying 'all the parents are complaining' (about what his particular complaint is about). Do not concede an inch.

I therefore put on a false smile and nodded encouragingly which obviously disconcerted him, used no doubt as he is to Mr. Chadband's thunderous rebuttal of his charges. Yes, he went on and asked, Did I not agree that it was a scandal that a teacher-of-all-people should order a child to assault another?

Inwardly agreeing that it was indeed scandalous, I nevertheless reflected on reports of little Vincent's chastened deportment
since the incident. And that the stupid Croser appeared inadvertently to have hit upon the exactly right treatment for him.

'Well,' he repeated. 'Isn't it a scandal and a disgrace?'

'Well,' I said playing for time, hoping that some succour
should be vouchsafed me and, as though in answer, my eye
caught Sir H. Newbolt's inspiring poem:

> The sand of the desert is sodden red
> The Gatling's jammed and the Colonel dead.

'How many strokes of the cane did you give the culprit?' he
asked, showing I thought considerable skill in 'When did you
last beat your wife' technique.

'That is my business,' I countered.

'Oh!' he said. 'You don't consider it *my* business then?'

Inwardly agreeing heartily that it was indeed his business,
I said, 'No.'

'In that case,' he said, 'I wish to punish the culprit myself.'

'Not on these premises,' I said.

He now lost his grip and began to bluster. I repeated that I
should investigate the incident.

'And then what?'

'That is my business.'

Realizing that we had come back to where we were originally,
he exclaimed in great rage, 'You have not heard the last of this.
You blasted teachers with your big pay and blasted long
holidays. I am going straight from here to the Education and I
am going to see it gets in all the papers.'

'Oh,' I said. 'Well, this is interesting. In that case, I might as
well send them the letter from Mr. Festing, the two from Mr.
Bull and also from Mr. Toseland all complaining of your son.
Then the Office can settle it between you and, if it gets in the
Sentinel, your neighbours can read what we have had to put up
with uncomplainingly for years.' And risking all, I slapped down
the letters which I had written for Lucinda Bull's father, and the
one purporting to come from Mr. Toseland who cannot read,
which I concocted last night.

This shook him considerably and, mercifully, he scarcely
glanced at them while I fixed him with a pleasant but determined
smile. In fact all he could say (weakly) was 'You have not heard

the last of this,' before retreating in utter disorder. I felt confident that I had weathered the gale and worked off my tension by telling Croser that he could creep out of his hole now and that this was the last time I would carry the can for his fat-headed stupidity.

This is Harpole the professional, in a situation which separates the men from the boys. In a hopeless position, untenable to all but devotees of Sir H. Newbolt's poetry, he takes the view that he is paid his extra allowance as Acting Head to protect even Croser whom he plainly detests. One must reluctantly agree that Slope has indeed a case, yet even the ranks of Tuscany can scarce forbear to cheer at Harpole's quite unreasonable refusal to back down an inch.

And what shining proof of the value of Record Cards from which each teacher can find solace and counsel from those further back along the child conveyor belt!

SLOPE TO ALDERMAN J. RAMSAY MACDONALD
DACRE, J.P.

(Complaint as before but suitably rephrased.)

DACRE TO SLOPE

This is an administrative matter that is sub-judice and I do not propose to deal with it. You should address this matter to the Education Offices.

SLOPE TO DACRE

You on the council are all the same – big-headed snobs. Wait till you come crawling down our street for a vote and you will get an earful.

DACRE TO SLOPE

I am an alderman and therefore will never need your vote again and you should watch your words my man.

SLOPE TO SIR EMRYS JENKINS, M.P.

(Complaint as before.)

SIR EMRYS JENKINS, M.P.'S SECRETARY TO SLOPE

Sir Emrys and Lady Jenkins are on a fact-finding mission in the Bahamas and will be away for some time. I have passed on your complaint to the Ombudsman.

OMBUDSMAN TO SLOPE

As apparently you are unaware, Parliament specifically placed complaints about the Civil Service and the workings of Local Government outside my terms of reference. You should therefore address your complaint to a representative of your County Education Committee.

SLOPE TO THE TAMPLING *Evening Sentinel*

(Complaint as before.)

Evening Sentinel TO SLOPE

Our legal department advises us that the letter sent by you under the nom-de-plume, 'Free Englishman', may be libellous. We therefore return it and suggest you address your complaint to a councillor or the member of parliament for this constituency who can refer it to the Ombudsman.

SLOPE TO HARPOLE

I have now sent full reports of your conduct to a county alderman, my M.P., the Ombudsman and the local press. So don't think you have got away with it.

Can Slope, can anyone, still be so ingenuous to believe that justice can be found in England by merely writing *for it?*

48

8

You seem unnaturally interested in our Harpole. Now for goodness sake get it into your silly head that if I mention him in our correspondence it merely is because I am thrown upon his company between 9 and 4 each and every day. If there is anything unusual about him it's his usualness. He has dragged himself up three rungs of what he imagines to be a social ladder and clings there, licking the boots stamping on his fingers . . . The zenith of his hopes is a semi with the mortage paid off, an adoring wife and enough pension at the end of it all to preserve life and threadbare respectability. And to achieve this he's prepared to put up with any indignity his superiors offload over him.

I grudgingly admit him a sort of integrity and if one shd have the misfortune to find oneself where the sands of the desert are running red and the gatling jammed and the colonel dead, there conceivably might be worse backs to be back to back with than Corporal Harpole's back.

But occasionally I *do* reflect that there *may* be another Harpole beneath the layers of servility. Such an occasion was last Saturday when netting newts with Henrietta and Titus in the Elver bordering Tampling Cricket Ground. Through a bank of willows whom shd I espy but G. Harpole at the wicket, fully armed and accoutred and looking larger than when in school, the light of battle glittering in his eye and rocketing balls into the spreading chestnut trees, paying particular attention to the offerings of Edward Muttler, only son of the local magnate, who was playing for the other side. I watched fascinated until he was outed in a most extraordinary fashion. Edward bowls a bouncer and our Harpole rears up on his toes, raises his bat like a club and hammers the ball like a thunderbolt at a little man who raises his hands either for mercy or protection. In vain! He is struck down like one dead, the missile bounding off his head to

49

drop gently into the hands of a neighbour. Whereupon G. Harpole, instead of rushing forward with healing in his wings, flings down his weapon with a godlike cry of rage and raises denunciatory arms to heaven at being thus outed. But, almost immediately, he resumes the old Harpole, begins apologizing busily all round and even helps drag his victim into the hut.

JOURNAL

Mrs. Grindle-Jones brought disturbing news this morning, an H.M.I. having visited her husband's establishment to see how they were fulfilling their statutory obligation to carry out Religious Instruction. She did not give details of what happened but plainly Grindle-Jones has been considerably discomfited by the visitation, she letting slip that the Inspector would be returning in a month's time. This speaks for itself.

Decided to investigate our own R.I. arrangements and, if necessary, to make adjustments before we have a similar inspection.

Tuesday
Miss Tollemache – Backward Class. Keeps repeating 'Jesus loves us.' Told the children 'He is waiting for us beyond the Bright Blue Sky where we shall sit at His feet and praise Him.' Then followed a detailed geographical description, particularly the vegetation. 'The palms there are not in pots as you may have seen at seaside hotels,' she said. 'These heavenly palms grow out of the ground.' 'No matter how much our mothers love us, Jesus loves us more,' she said. 'He sees our every action and knows our every thought so we must be careful what we *think*. When we do good things he is *happy* and when we do bad things he is *sad*. We should not like to make him *sad*, children, should we?' 'No, Miss Tollemache!' they chorused. Then, looking excessively pious, they all sprang to their feet and rattled off:

> 'Jesus loves us. This I know
> For the Bible tells me so.
> He doth count me with his sheep
> In his fold when I'm asleep.

Yea, Jesus loves me, Yea, Jesus loves me,
        Yea, Jesus loves me,
    The Bible tells me so.'
The Inspector should be satisfied with this.

Wednesday
Miss Foxberrow – Class 4.

When I entered, she immediately stopped. 'I should like to
observe your scripture lesson if I may,' I said. 'Oh well,' she
replied ungraciously, 'on your head be it. We are not grinding
our way through the Agreed Syllabus and you might as well
know this as we consider it a lot of brain-wash suitable only for
Nomadic Man.' 'Now children,' she said, 'I will continue this
demonstration lesson in which I shall use the well known
Deduction Method of Teaching because Mr. Harpole has come
to inspect me. As I was saying, if the Vicar died and Jesus
applied for the vacant post, do you think he would get the job?'
Several children answered affirmatively. 'You are wrong,' said
Miss Foxberrow. 'At 30, he would have been considered too
young. Then, of course, he was Working Class, didn't have a
degree, had not attended theological college and no doubt
spoke in a strong local dialect. And, let's face it, since Israel is a
very dusty place, he must have looked like a tramp . . .'

'Or a hippy,' Titus Fawcett interjected. 'Like the ones driven
off the sands at the seaside by ratepayers . . .'

'Yes, like a hippy, especially as his hair is believed to have
been long,' went on Miss Foxberrow. 'And we must remember
that he had no money, knew nobody who could pull the right
strings and had withdrawn from gainful employment. And we
must remember that he was not white; in fact some might have
called him coloured.'

She then turned a knowing eye on me and calmly asked,
'Supposing Jesus arrived by bus in Tampling St. Nicholas, what
do you think he would do?'

'Go to church!' called some of the duller children.

'You, Titus?' she asked, still looking fixedly at me. However,
feeling it unwise to become further implicated in what was near-
blasphemy, I unobtrusively withdrew to Mrs. Grindle-Jones's
room.

Bible in hand, she was reassuringly dictating notes on the
Prophet Amos.

I then was delighted to find Mr. Pintle's class making beautifully tinted maps of The Holy Land in the Times of the Prophet Amos.

As there was considerable noise in Croser's room he did not hear my entry, being seated at his desk studying his Bible. When he found me at his elbow he looked utterly confused which is understandable as he was gloating over an erotic passage in the Song of Solomon. He immediately began to shuffle through the pages.

'Please sir, can we take out our crayons and draw something as you usually let us whilst you're finding the place?' Vincent Slope called out cunningly.

'Stay in at playtime and write out Psalm 23,' Croser snapped mechanically.

His eye then lighted on something which inspired him and he boomed,

> 'Benaiah, the son of Jehoida, went down
> and slew a lion in a pit on a snowy day.'

'Ah,' he said. 'Now as a special treat I will tell you about the Great Prophet Benaiah, one of the best known warriors in the Old Testament.' He then carefully wrote a time-consuming B-E-N-A-I-A-H on the board. 'When this Benaiah was at school he could fight all the other boys in the playground and, of course, was a top monitor. He had everything laid out ready for his teacher at nine o'clock and frequently brought him sacrifices such as flowers and fruit.'

He nudged over towards me and whispered, 'You may think my approach is unusual, but they taught us at training college to convert everything to a child's own idiom. That is what I am doing.'

'In the evening he delivered newspapers and mowed lawns so that he could buy coal for his aged mother and pipe tobaccco for his aged father. Of course he passed the Eleven Plus. When he left grammar school (where he had been a prefect) he worked for the King as a Civil Servant. One day this King was in Big Trouble. "Find me a real tough man for a real tough job," he called. "A man who does not smoke, drink, swear or sap his strength in any other unseemly manner as there is a lion needs killing." Now, outside, it was the Hungry Season and was snowing hard, but Benaiah turned his back on the party he was

52

at, the buffet and free bar and dancing girls and he put on his skis and . . .'

The bell rang.

'I'll finish it tomorrow,' Croser said. 'Get out your mental books. If one car has 4 wheels how many wheels will 28 cars have? The steering wheel doesn't count.'

Went away feeling unusually depressed.

CIRCULAR TO ALL STAFF

The subject laid down for this week in the Agreed Syllabus of Religious Instruction is the Prophecy of the Prophet Amos and this should be taught. Failure to do so will be a teacher's individual responsibility should an H.M.I. visit.

Please sign this notice.

OFFICIAL LOG BOOK

Reminded the staff of the Provisions of the 1944 Education Act concerning their duties to follow a course of study as laid down in the Agreed Syllabus.

JOURNAL

Was inspecting the toilets, Theaker mutinously trailing behind me, when a child came and said a man was outside waiting to see me. I hurriedly checked that the visitor's car was the red Triumph 2000 we had been warned about and took the usual steps – each teacher receiving and then passing on a red marking pencil.

As I approached he said, 'Cole, H.M.I.' and I replied fatuously, 'Oh, I don't think we've met before.'

'I'm *sure* that we haven't,' he said, cleverly putting himself at advantage.

'Have you come about the R.I. ?' I asked.

'No,' he said, as though astonished. 'Why should I? I have merely come to wish you well during your term-in-charge and to ask you to call me in if difficulties arise.'

53

I escorted him to his car and, just before he got in, he looked carefully around and seeing we were alone, said, 'About R.I., Harpole . . . I remain unconvinced that it does a ha'porth of good. In fact, it is my belief that Christian Faith is best demonstrated to our children in the way a school lives, in its charity, kindness, helpfulness, cheerful vigour and constant seeking to increase the intellectual, emotional and spiritual potential of each person within it, if that doesn't sound too much like a quotation The Lord loves maths well taught. But I should not like to be quoted.'

I considered this quite significant and made an immediate note of it on the back of an envelope.

OFFICIAL LOG BOOK

Mr. G. B. Cole, H.M.I., arrived on a routine call at 9.15 a.m. and left at 9.23 a.m.

9

Had a request from Pintle that Titus Fawcett should be referred to the educational psychologist. He has Fawcett (Class 4) each a.m. from 9.30 to 10.30 in his Maths set and claims that he is surly and responsive neither to blame nor praise. (This particularly upsets him.) I agreed to do so but added that I had never known any good to come from this procedure as psychologists only regurgitate in their own jargon what you know already.

HARPOLE TO MISS GUDGEON, COUNTY COUNCIL
PSYCHOLOGIST

We are concerned about:

> Titus Fawcett
> Chronological age – 10 years 6 mnths.

We should appreciate you having a look at him and giving your expert opinion. His teacher finds him anti-social.

PSYCHOLOGIST'S REPORT ON TITUS FAWCETT

> Chronological age – 10 years 6 mnths
> Mental age   – 15 years 4½ mnths.

Any behavioural difficulties in school almost certainly due to under-employment of highly developed mental ability. Should be given opportunity to proceed at own speed.

JOURNAL

Incredulous at report on T. Fawcett. Pintle said sourly, 'Well, if that's all the ratepayers get for her £3,000 a year! She ought to see his slovenly handwriting.'

Rang Miss Gudgeon who assured me that there was no mistake in her report and that the boy was 'a near genius'. She suggested that it would be most interesting if I investigated his family to discover if it was inherited ability and that the result would make 'a nice little monograph for our *Institute of Education Quarterly*'. Decided to pursue this as publication in a learned journal might further my career and, finding myself with no routine tasks and knowing the boy's father was on Nights at the Sewage Works, I sent for him.

He slunk in, sank back into the armchair and closed his eyes. Were you personally a good scholar? I asked him. No, he said, I was Anything But. I hated my teachers and my teachers hated me.

All of them? I asked amazed. All, he replied. They never studied me so I never studied them.

Tell me about your schooldays, I said. I can't, he said. I have dismissed them from my mind as an encumbrance.

Why, Mr. Fawcett, I said stiffly. You can't do: it is impossible. Not at all, he said. The human mind has but a limited capacity and we must not cram it with junk and rubbish.

That is sheer nonsense, I said with some heat. You cannot compare the human brain, with its infinite possibilities, to a box room.

That is as it may be, he said. But it is not *my* opinion. Nor was it my Dad's.

Well, let us agree to disagree, I said. As we are getting away from what I wanted to see you about, which was your son, Titus, and why the County Psychologist says he is so bright. Let me ask you first what newspapers you read? I don't read one, he said.

Why don't you? I demanded, pointing out that everybody else read newspapers. He said, They alarm and disturb me with all these wars, strikes and murders and humanity at strife. But if you don't know what is going on in Tampling and the rest of the world, how can you converse with your mates at work? I asked, getting near the end of my patience. I don't talk to them, he said. I sit apart for my snap. I don't heed them and they don't heed me. Well, I said, we are getting away from my investigation again. Let us go further back still. To *your* father. Oh, he said, you will get nowhere on that tack as it was him who passed it on to me. He counselled me, If you want to stay free from bother

56

and calm in mind, read nothing except food-tin labels and your rent-book.

Then *his* father? I said (beginning to wonder how all this rigmarole could be made significant for a learned journal). Ah, he said, with a glimmer of interest, if our Titus is bright as you say he is then it is my little old Grandad he gets it from as he is called after him, he himself being called after the last great King of Rome. Oh, at last! I said sarcastically. Then *he* was a good scholar? No, he said, if you call good scholars them who can read, write and figure because he couldn't do any of that as I've been told. This being because he never settled in one place long enough having no home as he could say was his. He lived with a very big woman who was not his wife. And I have heard *she* was a very educated woman with many talents whose father was nobility and they used to walk from one place to the next, she carrying all the kit, and never slept twice in the same spot these being stables, barns, woods and stacks.

This was more rewarding, so I asked, Did they not become ill from exposure to the weather? No, he said, they wore many sets of clothes, each a bit bigger than the layer below it and so the rain never got down to their skins. They never took off these clothes and they never lay down as they knew how to sleep sitting.

Well, my head was full of questions about personal hygiene, but I restricted my curiosity to enquiring how his grandfather managed to beget his father if he never removed his garments? It was an angel did it, Mr. Fawcett said.

Well, I was very disappointed with the turn my enquiry had taken, as, frankly, I could see no university journal would ever print this nonsense however much I edited it.

What happened to this remarkable pair? I asked him. Ah, he said, that is very interesting as they died in a hedge-bottom under a briar bush and I have seen the place. There was a farm labourer passing by on his bike and Grandad calls 'What time is it mate?' And he answers, 'Six o'clock mate.' So my Grandad asks him what was the date and the year and he tells him that as well. Then Grandad nodded at this woman, who was Titus's Great-Grandma in a roundabout way, and they smiles each at the other and then they took hold of each other's hands and leaned back into the bush and passed on.

Have you ever told Titus this? I asked. Why yes, he said. I

have related it to him many times because as we have no papers or books we have plenty of time for talk and society and this is a source of pleasure and profit to the both of us . . .

Well, thank you very much, I said. That certainly clears up a few things for me and I feel it safe to tell you that your son will pass the Eleven Plus with ease. Then he went.

This is encouraging because it shows Harpole as a sympathetic listener, a prime though rare qualification in head-teachers. Ridiculous as are Fawcett's folk memories of his ancestor, Harpole has not wasted his time because a talker transfers his self-approbation to his audience. Thus Harpole can feel sure that, in any future encounters with Titus in anti-social mood, Fawcett père, whilst not siding with the school, will at least maintain benevolent neutrality.

Furthermore, Harpole has widened his terms of reference by not confining his influence and interest to the school alone. All good schoolmasters, through the ages, have been powers for good in their community, knowing education to leaven all it touches.

JOURNAL

Sitting quietly in The Fusilier when, not at all to my pleasure, Shutlanger joined me and began to bind on about a horse called The Fairy. 'He was 'b****y pulled,' he kept repeating, 'The b*****d pulled him.' He was in the middle of this when to my astonishment I saw Miss Foxberrow not as usual in her long cloak but in a very becoming Liberty silk frock which fitted her tightly which I found disturbing. She was sitting with her head very close to Edward Muttler who, as usual, was wearing a very expensive suit and they were laughing.

Shutlanger must have noticed my preoccupation because he said in a vulgarly carrying whisper, 'Who is that chick with the marvellous ***s? I could go over her with a tape measure.' I am convinced that Miss F. heard him because she looked around very amused and put a restraining hand on the arm of Muttler who, to do him credit, started to rise belligerently to his feet. I tried to distract Shutlanger's attention by asking him if he had heard from his wife but, though this normally throws him into a self-pitying passion, he continued to stare lecherously at Miss Foxberrow and to mutter into his moustache.

As they left, I affected not to notice but she called 'Good-night, Mr. Harpole,' in a loud voice and they went off in his Aston Martin.

'Oh so you *****y know her,' said Shutlanger coarsely, and when I told him she was on my staff he said, 'Well if she was on *my* staff I'd have her helping me tidy up my little stockroom in her free periods.'

10

Sitting in The Fusilier listening to Shutlanger's maunderings I asked myself however he managed to rise to be the Grammar School Headmaster, lacking as he does scholarship, presence and an acceptable moral code. I rephrased these thoughts less hurtfully and asked him.

'Oh,' he smirked, 'it was easy. Just exploitation of Human Nature. The trouble with you, Harpole, is that you credit the human race with too much virtue and intelligence. And this will always keep you in the less successful segment of Society. If you want to know, I rose *on the back of a castle.*'

'Put your fingers over your eyes,' he went on and, when I had done so, asked 'Is it all dark? Well, that was like (*a*) my first classroom and (*b*) my spirits when my first headmaster, a pitiless man, pushed me into it. You could take in Olde Tyme England without stirring from your desk. This cave smelled like a mouldering hassock, the gasbracket leaked and whenever the door banged, whitewash fell like scurf. The last tenant (receiving a Breakdown Pension) had left his litter – torn bills urging SAVE FOR SECURITY, a folio of his cave-man drawings of Our Friends the Birds and a grocer's box smelling abominably of diseased rabbits called PETS CORNER.

'But Harpole,' he went on, 'and grapple this to your heart with hoops of steel – it is Always darkest before the Dawn, the Seeds of Victory are sown in Defeat etc. My gaze fell upon a *Norman Castle* perching crazily on top of a cupboard. A draught was rocking its keep, discoloured paste gaped from its ramparts, the drawbridge was tacked on with stamp-edging. Lesser men would have rammed it immediately into the waste basket. Not me. Instead, I reflected, What lesson can this pitiable object teach?

'Now Harpole, I am going to question you. At your training

college (long ago but not, I trust, forgotten) what did they advise you to have your class make when you *did* the Romans?' 'A chariot,' I said mechanically. 'Right,' he said. 'And for the Danes?' 'A longship,' I replied. (After all, this is well known – everybody does it.) 'And when you *did* the Normans? Don't answer – I can read it in your eye. Well, I thought, there must be a thousand of these primitive fortresses decaying gently on cupboard tops up and down Britain. And Inspectors and Officials who carry preferment in their pockets must be sick of the sight of them. So if I am ever to escape into a headmaster's cosy nest, it behoves me to be Different.

'My form was a C streamer, dull, brutish and utterly un-appreciative of the 1870 Public Education Act. The Salt Mines was the place for them and, in a properly organized state, most of them would only have been allowed up for air on Christmas Day.' He said this with such a degree of ferocity that I could see he still remembered that form. In fact, for a time he was lost in thought, quite literally grinding his teeth . . .

'So, I bought a big bag of cement and two more of sand and, whenever one of these brutes gave me offence, I detained him and compelled him to mix concrete and cast it into small blocks two inches in length and one inch in depth. Other offenders mortared the blocks into walls: my Castle grew. Like all conquerors I had my setbacks because this novel and tedious punishment so broke their degraded spirits that even I couldn't find reasonable excuses for detaining them. So I took options on malefactors from other forms and my popularity with the staff rose conversely as it diminished with the boys. Productivity rose again. Parents complained, some about the near-suicidal gloom of their sons, others of their unnatural weariness and, a particularly ingenious one, a civil servant, reported me to the Ministry of Town and Country Planning. (This failed because no regulation forbidding the erection of a dwelling inside a dwelling could be found.)

'My Castle no longer stood: it *loomed*. If ever walls could be said to frown, these did. One of the staff, an embittered, unsuccessful man, said that it was true to history in one respect at least – it had been founded upon tears and misery.

'I can truthfully say that it is the only thing in Education which has truly absorbed me. Looking back, I realize it was not me: it was another man. People looked at me oddly, my opinions

61

were deferred to: the Head, who plainly had come to protest, stayed to feign admiration. In the end, the obsession transferred to the boys themselves. It was incredible – they worked voluntarily and I found I had become tremendously popular.'

'Yes,' I said. 'But what did it lead to?'

'Cast your bread upon the waters etc.,' he said complacently. 'And that's a true saying and worthy to be believed, Harpole. An Inspector came, a little, bent woman. She edged gingerly into my room and gazed at my Castle. She was silent for a very long time. Then, in awed tones, she said, "Mr. Shutlanger, *what triumph for the Montessori Method*! The children have been *living* History!"

'Three months later I was appointed to a Post of Responsibility in a forward-looking school: my foot was on the 2nd rung.'

'But what about the Castle?' I asked him.

'It was built to last,' he said confidently. 'It must still be there. No doubt my successors keep rabbits in it.'

Even discounting much of this as in vino non veritas, *Shutlanger's account of his blast-off to higher planes of preferment by no means is as fantastic as it may sound. There is little to choose between half the applications for teaching posts: if one plays a piano, another plays rugger for Penzance-Newlyn and another has dug wells for a year in Muscat. Education officers and governors are human: it is the unusual they remember . . .*

FREE WRITING BY TITUS FAWCETT

Last night after school we played Lower End School in the 1st round of the Cricket Shield and we got knocked out. I don't think it was fair and all the others don't think it was fair as well. We won the toss and put them in and we got two of them out in the first over and hit another on the head. And we had five of them out all clean bowled and they had scored only three runs. Then the next over we outed two more and each time their headmaster who was umpiring shouted No Ball after the wickets were down and also when one of them knocked his bails off with his own bat their headmaster said it was the wind blew them off when there wasn't a wind blowing. And then when Mr. Harpole was umpiring at the other end we got two of them out again but he said he couldn't hear the snick of the one we caught and that he couldn't be sure that the one who we hit on the legs was hiding all his wickets. Mr. Harpole is over fair and to prove it these same two of them ran into each other and lay knocked out in the middle of the pitch but Mr. Harpole would not let us run both or even one of them out because he said it wouldn't be sporting. But their headmaster gave 8 wides and 13 no-balls and got their score up to 27 and he was always shouting at them when to run and when not to run and where to hit the ball and when to block it.

When it came to our innings we got 25 for five and would have won easy but their headmaster gave five of us out in one over when he was at the right end, three for leg before, one for picking up the ball to throw it back to the bowler and he said I was out for obstruction because I shouted Drop it at one of their fielders and he did. I am never going to play cricket again as it is too easy for cheating and injustice which upsets me like it does our dad.

Too much significance should not be read into this harrowing account of a headmaster's love for his school. Similar temptation has been too much for many another upright man who, only a few hours before, had urged the pursuit of Righteousness in his Daily Service.

CROSER TO HARPOLE

The insect enclosed in the matchbox has been sent to me for identification. I have looked it up in all the ref. books and it is not there. Can you oblige and tell me what it is?

HARPOLE TO CROSER

I do not know what it is either. Tell him it is a very *rare* one and that he should take it down to the Museum. Give him a house point.

... a boy Geoffrey Lowestoft showed me a creature in a matchbox which he said his grandad had captured and which was very valuable because his teacher, the Abominable Croser, had told him that this was the first specimen ever found in England as its home is the deep Congo bush and must have been brought here in a crate of yams. It was a very plump thing so I asked what he fed it on and he said that it had been like that since capture and actually was growing thinner. By this time I was in a state of near hysterics (but concealed it) as the thing was nothing but a Common Bed Bug and plainly was sleeping off a massive meal on one of the Lowestofts. I told him it was *Sentrium Nocturnalis*, otherwise the Greater Night Watchman, and in the morning I had a letter from his grandad thanking me for identifying it and that he had found another and was going to breed them as a hobby.

MR. GRINDLE-JONES TO MISS FOXBERROW, M.A.
(Cantab.)

I am arranging my programme for next winter for my Parent-Teacher Association and as my wife tells me that you are keen on Local History I wonder if you can be prevailed upon to give us a talk on an aspect of it. My parents, with one or two notable exceptions, are not an intellectual lot so perhaps something on the lighter side would be appropriate or history of a romantic nature in which our County abounds – local apparitions, elopements and the like. There is a good bus from Melchester leaving at 7.10 p.m. and I shall arrange to drive you home afterwards.

MISS FOXBERROW TO MR. GRINDLE-JONES

I feel that an isolated lecture on such a large subject serves no useful purpose so I must decline your kind invitation. However, if you care to suggest to your committee that, after a brief preliminary talk, I should lead a discussion on A Village School's Role in its Community, I should be delighted to come. And, as I believe parents should take a much more positive part in educational policy-making, I should hope to persuade your P.T.A. to send a resolution to the County Education Committee urging that the preponderance of Managers of primary schools should be parents of children attending school and that any person who sends his/her children to a fee-paying school should be debarred membership of local education committees.

MR. GRINDLE-JONES TO MISS FOXBERROW

I feel you may have misunderstood the raison d'être of our little group and enclose last year's calendar of events to give you an idea of our activities.

September 30	Theatre Outing to see *The Mouse Trap*
November 15	Bring and Buy Olde Tyme Xmas Fayre for Colour T.V. Fund
January 4	Annual Dinner at The Crown, Melchester
February 18	Talk by Brigadier Lumley-Lampson, D.S.O., R.V.O., – 'Amritsar: I was there.'
March 10	Bring and Buy Olde Tyme Easter Fayre for Summer Educational Outing to Mablethorpe

Such a discussion as you suggest is really not our cup of tea so I feel it not worthwhile suggesting it to the committee.

CIRCULAR FROM HARPOLE TO STAFF

Each teacher has a list of children receiving free meals and will be notified by me of any names withdrawn or added. Thus it is quite unnecessary to summon children receiving free meals to your desks each Monday to tell you he/she is present and is eligible for free meals because you will already have marked the class register and need merely mark him/her in the meals register. I am sure there is no need for elaboration on the social reasons for asking you to follow this procedure.

PINTLE TO HARPOLE

My method of having *all* children eating school dinners, Paid or Free, line up at my desk ensures accurate accounting. If a Free Dinner Child doesn't consider that five free meals a week is worth the effort of saying the three words, 'Free Dinner, Sir' to me, an alternative is at hand – he or she can go home for the meal.

HARPOLE TO PINTLE

I have no doubt some children find it shameful to admit (because this is what it amounts to) that their father's low income puts them in the Free Meal category, and, as a teacher, I am sure that you will agree that a low income is often not a man's fault. Still less can a child be responsible for its own poverty. I should therefore be greatly obliged if you would put the new system into effect forthwith.

Yes, this is the right and proper thing. But why echo Pintle's jargon – he being an old hand at holding up progress by correspondence? One supposes Harpole is avoiding facing up to him.

JOURNAL

Passing down the corridor heard Pintle call out, 'Now the *Free* Dinners! *Free* Dinners line up at my desk so I can check you.' Felt enraged beyond bounds, shot in and invited Pintle somewhat unceremoniously into the corridor and there hissed, 'I have told you what I want done. *Do it*!', glaring fiercely at him. He went red and for once failed to argue the point.

I shall be glad when Mr. Chadband comes back.

11

Just before morning bell rang I happened to pass Miss Tollemache's room and, glancing in, saw a most morbid occurrence
being enacted. From a Sainsbury carrier bag she removed a
withered wreath and hung it on a nail adjacent to her wall
blackboard. Decided not to act precipitously.

*Harpole evidently remembers from his Registration Crusade that
Miss Tollemache needs to be handled like a live bomb. This
harmless eccentric would be far better allowed to go her own ways
but, knowing Harpole's zealous pursuit of the good and true,
this hardly seems likely.*

HARPOLE TO EDITH WARDLE

... Decided that subtlety was called for, so dropped in during
morning play apropos of nothing and asked a passing child to
bring us two cups of tea. After praising the needlework samplers
her class have been toiling at since last September, I indicated
the wreath and said in an airy manner, 'Ah, I see the children
have brought you some flowers. What a pity they have withered.
I'll take them away for you because, as it happens, I shall be
passing the dustbins.'
  'Oh,' she said, 'thank you very much but no thank you,'
adding cryptically, 'There is a flower that bloometh when
autumn leaves are fled, tis the Memory of the Past,' (a quotation
from the Poets). My immediate reaction was to insist on its
instant removal but was uncertain of my legal position. This
thing is beginning to obsess me.

Most confidential
I question that the case you instance comes under my aegis.
There may be merit in your assertion that superstition impinges
up to a point. However I disclaim competence to adjudge this.
In delicate matters such as this one is, personal susceptibilities
might be offended. Have you sought guidance *Elsewhere*?

I must request that this letter be treated in *Strictest Confidence*.

TUSKER TO HARPOLE

I am surprised that this trivial matter has been referred to me.
This is purely an internal matter of routine on which it is not my
duty to offer advice.

N.U.T. COUNTY SECRETARY TO HARPOLE

I take your point but you would be well advised to take no
action unless you can show what you believe to be a funeral
wreath is verminous and likely to be injurious to health. An
objection to its presence merely on metaphysical grounds would
be difficult to sustain. Have you considered consulting the
Diocesan Director of Education?

JOURNAL

Visited Miss Tollemache's classroom and, after ascertaining
that Theaker was at the other end of the building, closely
examined the wreath. I shook it but no dust or vermin were
dislodged. In fact it appeared to be in unusually good condition
and without odour.

In casual conversation with children, I learnt that, besides the
usual milk, needlework, pencil, painting etc. monitors, there is a
Special Flower Monitor whose duty it is to 'gently' dust *it* each
second day.

All else having failed, decided to come right out with it.
'*Must* you have that wreath in your classroom?' I said.

'I *must*,' she said, 'and I will tell you why. It symbolises the graveyard of the bright hopes I once had of being given a proper class like everybody else. Ever since I came here, which was before even Mr. Chadband, I have been landed with "The Backwards." There was a time when, in my ignorance, I felt only sorry for *myself*. But now it is for them – "The Backwards"! I have come to abhor Streaming: it shows such a crude lack of respect. They know what C means alright – even before A's and B's and disappointed parents translate it. We teach children not to complain, so all they've left is to cry into their pillow and, when they're big enough, kick in the windows of telephone booths. I did think when *you* took over that you'd abolish it.' I went away utterly astonished and chastened.

CIRCULAR TO STAFF

The Backward Class will cease to exist on Friday at 4 p.m. The normal practice of a child spending one year in each teacher's class is a mere conventionality. Thus, since we now have 5 teachers for 4 classes, I propose that, in their first three years in the school, each teacher shall pass on the children after 27 weeks. Because of the Eleven Plus, the top class will not be affected by this arrangement.

And whilst 2X is destroyed by this crashing pronunciamento, Chadband is fiddling with a tambourine or even a triangle!

12

I have long known that Theaker only speaks either to complain or gloat. 'Them Widmerpools is being shifted by the Council into that empty house down by the sewerage that's all on its own as the neighbours won't pay their rents until they're moved on,' he informed me. Although I assumed a look of utter unconcern, I could tell from his face that he was not dissatisfied at the effect of the dread announcement.

This is catastrophic. This family is famed throughout the town for its utter lack of social responsibility, their numerous progeny roaming abroad all hours of day and night, leaving a trail of havoc in their wake, so that they are shunned and feared by all respectable ratepayers.

JOURNAL

D Day. Mrs. Widmerpool, a fat, jovial woman followed by 7 offspring turned up. 'You can't have 'em all, love,' she said. 'Three's for the Infants and there's four more at the Secondary.'

All the children gathered round me and stared curiously up, no doubt assessing how far they dare go.

Fortunately, they had not obtained a Transfer Form from North End so I refused to accept them. Oddly enough, she neither argued nor lost her temper but stumped off saying she'd try her luck at the Infants.

This is Harpole at his lowest ebb. He must know that movement from one school to another in the same small town does not really require a Transfer Form and obtaining one can only delay the Widmerpool invasion by 24 hours.

*And why should he be astonished that Mrs. Widmerpool takes
her rebuff calmly? Does he suppose he is the only official who has
practised bloody-mindedness on such as her? She has learnt from
experience that there is always a higher official to carve up a
lower one. How much more constructive and better for future
relations if Harpole had dissimulated and expressed delight at the
opportunity of meeting this famed child-bearer and her brood and,
in their presence, extracting from her a blanket approval of any
future chastisement he may decide necessary for their moral
regeneration.*

R. W. JUDD, HEADMASTER, NORTH END C.P. SCHOOL TO HARPOLE

I have heard from a certain source that you are trying to dodge
having the Widmerpools. I enclose all the relevant forms and
papers for transfer and, as far as I am concerned, they no longer
exist. I take a dim view of this and shall draw it to Mr. Chadband's attention on his return. It has always been an unwritten
rule amongst local *head-teachers* that we take the rough with
the smooth.

EXTRACT FROM RECORD CARD TRANSFERRED FROM TAMPLING NORTH END C.P.

'... father and mother unco-operative. Children wilful,
deceitful, uniformly low mentally. *April* – 2 oldest boys broke
into school but unable to prove it, forced open 3 teachers'
drawers, head-teacher's cash-box, needlework money taken.
August – Fire started in 3C classroom by Widmerpools but
Police said insufficient evidence ...'

			yrs.		yrs.
Vanessa Widmerpool	Chronological Age		11.3	Reading Age	7.0
Reuben	,,	,,	10.1	,, ,,	6.5
Matthew	,,	,,	9.0	,, ,,	5.8
Ringo	,,	,,	8.2	,, ,,	5.0

HARPOLE TO TUSKER

I have received transfer forms in respect of Vanessa, Reuben,

Matthew and Ringo Widmerpool from North End Primary School.

As accommodation here is limited, would it be possible for this family to continue attendance at their present school until suitable vacancies occur here? I understand that the children are very happy there and it might be injurious to their educational advance to move them at this juncture.

TUSKER TO HARPOLE

I am deeply concerned at your assumption that St. Nicholas enjoys special status amongst the town's primary schools. I am not aware of the 'limited accommodation' at St. Nicholas and it certainly has no *de facto* meaning since neither the Department of Education nor our local authority has set a limit on the number of children who can be accommodated in a primary school. You may assume that there are *always* vacancies.

Please admit the Widmerpools immediately.

JOURNAL

Feeling that I had taken all reasonable precautions against being landed with the Widmerpools, resolved to make the best of a bad job, they having been deposited outside the office by their mother who, to give her credit, showed no sign of triumph. I examined them with the greatest attention and came to the conclusion that children with such knowing eyes, allied with Judd's record of their cunning, could be taught to read. Immediately set in train a crash course, ordering that the 1st and 2nd should sit in the library from 9.30 until 12 and 1.30 – 3.30 each day and read solidly through the Janet & John Infant Reading Course Books 1–4, going twice through each book and its supplementaries. These would be in charge of a rota of advanced children from Class 4. Meanwhile, I positioned the 3rd and 4th Widmerpools outside the office with instructions to ask me to hear each three pages they had prepared and to have them ticked-off.

Had scarcely turned my back when Ringo, the 4th Widmerpool, seized the school brass hand-bell and began to ring it loudly. When I emerged he grinned defiantly and threw it the length of the corridor, causing Pintle and Mrs. Grindle-Jones to rush from their rooms and stare unbelievingly at the scene – our brass bell being as sacroscanct as the Holy Grail. He then fled homewards while his brothers and sister broke into loud and mocking laughter, from which I deduced that they had witnessed similar scenes before.

Feeling that this was a Crise de Confidence, I immediately set off in pursuit on my bicycle. When he saw me, his expression changed from exultation to alarm and, realising that, at my greater speed, I must surely head him off, he doubled in his tracks. I therefore ran my bike against a privet hedge and took up the chase on foot. His panic was now such that he dashed into the garden of a semi-detached and, being cornered, fled for sanctuary into the house itself so that we both burst into the kitchen where a young woman was doing the washing.

She was too amazed to cry out so, seizing the 4th Widmerpool and lifting him kicking and writhing under my arm, I raised my hat and withdrew. During the struggle his braces burst and he lost one shoe.

By now, several indignant householders had come into their front gardens, calling encouragement to the 'poor little chap' and denouncing me. Nevertheless, knowing that it was for his ultimate good, keeping a firm grip on his collar, I marched him off, he being too preoccupied with hopping and keeping up his trousers to resist further. With some difficulty I simulated a pleasant smile and nodded at the outraged onlookers.

I then assembled the other chastened Widmerpools and, placing the 4th one over my knees, gave him four hearty smacks with Janet & John Bk. III (which is a hardback). This reawakened his bawling and visibly impressed the others. Feel that I have made a good start with the reformation of this new family in my care.

EMMA FOXBERROW TO FELICITY FOXBERROW

... During the past month there has been an extraordinary educational thing going on here. A family called Widmerpool, whose very name causes every right-minded citizen of Tampling to blench and dial 999, were admitted. G. Harpole, who does not appear to have read anything by educational experts, is still in a State of Nature. For instance, he believes juvenile law-lessness is caused by lack of self-esteem and that lack of self-esteem is caused by lack of success and lack of success is caused initially by inability to read. So four hapless kids were thrown into a merciless non-stop reading jag. You never saw such a change! From cheerful savages they have become punch-drunk automata. I swear their lips begin to sound out words if one *says* 'book.'

The staggeringly improbable thing is that it has worked. In 3 weeks they have been dragged shrieking into literacy and distributed to normal classes.

I mentioned this to G. Harpole. He said modestly, 'Oh, do you think so? It is very good of you to mention the matter. It *does* seem to work doesn't it? But I shouldn't like it spread around because, although I *know* being unable to read is the cause of moral collapse, I also know the Experts would make fun of me, particularly as I'm not a graduate of anywhere.'

JOURNAL

Feeling that the Widmerpool children were now well on the road to rehabilitation, I invited the parents to call on me. Only Mrs. W. came. '*He* won't get out of bed today,' she said, 'but he says if you will send which one has been giving trouble he will belt him.' I explained that the children were making excellent progress and I had merely asked their parents to call so that we could discuss the advantages of 'limiting' their family as, in my opinion, each new child impoverished the rest.

'Don't talk to me,' she said. 'I don't want any more. I didn't want the last three. He made me have 'em on Saturday nights. Not that now they're here I don't think the same of them as of the first six. He won't let me be and must always be having it which I like and I don't like, if that makes sense to you. What I mean is I shouldn't like it if he didn't want it some time. I have seen it in my sister's love-magazine that the well-off only has it of a week-end, but when I told *him* he said, "Well we'll go on as before and to keep up with the Joneses we'll have it twice on Sundays." ' She then said that she would see that he came round to hear what I had to say.

I therefore paved the way by sending Widmerpool a good

used suit from the Round Tablers which brought him round next day to complain it was too tight around the crutch. He is a large man but overweight and furtive and talks in a kind of hoarse whisper. 'If it's one of the kids,' he said, 'tell me which one and I'll have his hide, sir.'

I explained to him modern research had shown that, if he needed to chastise his children more than once after the age of three, he should reconsider his disciplinary methods, and then went on to say that I was concerned about his economic plight and told him each new child depressed his family's standard. He listened with great interest and agreed to accept the loan of *New Techniques of Married Love.*

'Well,' he wheezed, 'ta for this sex-book and you have not wasted a word on me, Sir, and what you have been saying is no more than I know to be proper but *she* has not told you the lot by a long chalk not she. She is never satisfied or never has been; in fact you can take it as gospel the older she grows the worse she gets, and if anybody has a grouse it is me not getting my proper rest. And then there is *him*, Sir.'

'Him!' I exclaimed, flabbergasted by this glimpse into the social life of the Poor.

'Yes,' he said, 'Alfred . . . I don't see why you shouldn't have a go at him as well as me, but he won't come to see you, sir, as he never shifts from the scullery, watching his chance.'

Visited the Widmerpool home and found 'Alfred', a large hairy man, almost submerged in drifts of washing.

'Ah!' he said, 'I have heard of you from the kids as they hold you in great respect. They are very good and learn me what you learn them and it takes me out of myself, and continually adds to my education.' When I apologized for visiting on Washing Day he said 'Every day except the Sabbath is Washing Day with eleven kids and the Mr. and Mrs.'

I remarked that it looked as though he could do with a washing machine. 'Oh no,' he said, 'I have seen them on the telly but it would not do for us as I wash complete rig-outs and, in a machine, the buttons would get split.'

'These new detergents must be a great boon,' I said. 'Oh,' he replied, 'I know of them from the telly – Omo, Daz, Fairy Snow and those new others that eat dirt. They are not for me – yellow soap and pounding is the best.'

75

'Well,' I said, 'to get to the point, I am concerned about the size of the family.' 'Yes,' he said, 'and I agree with you considering that every new one adds to the Washing. But what can I do? It is the Will of God that the kids keep coming just as it is His Will that I do the Washing. We all have our place in the Scheme of Things.'

'Yes,' I said sharply, 'that is all very well but there is the *human* element too. Babies are not flown-in by the stork,' adding sarcastically, 'I hope it is no secret from you that the procreative process requires the help of a man and a woman.'

'That may be,' he said, 'and I have no complaints. It is enough for me to get on with the Washing. Whatever the right and wrong of things in the world, *that*'s got to be got through.'

I was exasperated by his obtuseness by this time. 'It is not enough to bring children into the world,' I said. 'They must be cared for – and by that I don't mean just doing this washing.'

'That's over-big a thing for me,' he said, 'as I never had no Education. When my time comes, I have told the Mrs. that the National Health is not to be told, and the Hospital and the Crem is not to have me. And this she has vowed on a Bible. Till then, it is enough that I have the Washing.'

I was appalled at this narrow concept of life and went away feeling irritated at my wasted journey. From now on I will try to educate the three of them through the children.

13

No sooner arrived this morning than Mrs. Tusswell, dramatically holding herself in, appeared. News of her arrival must have come to the ears of Pintle, in whose class Chloe Tusswell is, because he turned up complaining about the quality of modern drawing pins but, in reality, to see if Mrs. Tusswell had come up about him. To my annoyance I had scarcely turned towards her, let alone spoken, when her face collapsed and she began weeping bitterly. 'Come, come,' I said. 'Whatever it is, it can't be as bad as all that!'

'It is, it is!' she cried. 'As I was combing Chloe's hair last night I found a lop, and then another. Fat grey ones, some crawling and some still eggs not hatched out. In fact, the head was alive with them. It was that awful I had the hysterics and didn't get a wink of sleep all night, so that Mr. Tusswell, my husband, went off downstairs on to the sitting-room settee in the finish and, when I followed him, he flew into a rage and swore at me, yelling that I was off my head and would drive him off his as well.' And remembrance of her wrongs started her off wailing again.

Having a temperamental defect which causes me to dislike weeping women, particularly big, powerful and overbearing women like Mrs. Tusswell, I was able to regard this performance impassively and even managed to get on rectifying several mistakes in Miss Tollemache's dinner register. Whereupon the abominable woman, noting my lack of attention, veered from self-pity to cries demanding vengeance. 'It's them Widmerpools,' she hissed, coming to the real purpose of her visit. 'Chloe was rubbed against by one of them yesterday and we want them seen to. And if you don't, some of us on the Estate are going to get up a Petition.'

'Oh,' I said coldly, 'and how can you know it's the

Widmerpools? Your child may have been touched by fifty children. This is a *school* you know. All the same I'll have the nurse inspect Chloe's class. And now I have some teaching to do.'

Verminous Infestation

I had today a visit from Mrs. Widmerpool of 111, Tollemache Way, complaining that you are threatening to have her children singled out for examination to ascertain whether or not infectious vermin are present on her children's scalps.

May I point out to you that discrimination of this nature is deplored by competent authorities as anti-social. Kindly let me have a report on what action you have taken.

HARPOLE TO MRS. WIDMERPOOL

What you have heard is quite untrue. As a matter of Routine, the whole school had its half-yearly Head Inspection and no children were singled out for special examination. Any children found by the nurse to have unclean heads were given a letter in a plain envelope. I understand you did not receive such a communication.

Why cannot *Harpole write in a friendly direct English to such people? This jargon identifies him with the army of humourless officials determined to maintain social fragmentation. He could just as easily have written:*

> *Dear Mrs. Widmerpool,*
> *Whatever gave you such an idea? In the interests of cleanliness the hair of every child in the school is inspected once a term by the nurse . . .*

but his scarcely forgivable error was in not repudiating much more vigorously Mrs. Tusswell's nomination of the Widmerpools as the offenders. Except in outrageously laudatory terms, it is fatal to even say aloud the name of one parent to another because the meaner-souled will barb the mildest utterance to pay off old scores.

78

Surely Harpole must know that the Widmerpools have brought
segregation on to his doormat, and that no-one is a more virulent
upholder of the English caste system than the woman who is just a
little less cast-out than the outcast?

JOURNAL

Mrs. Grindle-Jones brought two of her ten-year olds to me this
afternoon.

During a cutting-out lesson, one, Rodney Cleethorpes, had
snatched the shared pair of scissors and had cut a large snip in
his desk-mate's, the 2nd Widmerpool's, jersey. 'Because he
snipped my finger first, Sir,' exclaimed the accused child. After
reminding him that I was to be addressed as Mr. Harpole and
not as Sir ('I have not been knighted yet. Perhaps later though,'
I said jocularly), I examined the finger he held up and then, to
make absolutely sure, all his others but could find no evidence
of an incision. 'I sucked it better,' he admitted, and immediately
burst into tears.

So that Mrs. Grindle-Jones should report to her husband that
we took hooliganism seriously, I took the offender across my
knees and chastised him with the flat of my hand, unfortunately
not hardened appreciably being still early in the cricket season.
Mrs. G.-J. turned modestly away. I then told the second
Widmerpool to report to his mother that I was sorry about the
damage caused to his jersey but that he had seen me deal with
the matter, and dismissed them.

Mrs. Cleethorpes arrived at 9.55 a.m. as I was demonstrating to
half a dozen girls from Mr. Pintle's class how to ascertain the
capacity of a bucket. (Mr. Pintle still refuses to teach the New
Maths.) On seeing her I sent the children off to the toilets with
the bucket and some one-third pint milk bottles and, suppressing
my annoyance, invited the woman into my study and offered
her an easy chair. Although she looked surprisingly healthy she
told me she had not slept a wink last night worrying about
Rodney's future as his father wasn't worrying about Rodney's
conduct only in eating off the fat of the land and boozing with
his mates not that there was another woman mark you, and
Rodney's upbringing all fell on her shoulders and she was a

good wife and mother as all the neighbours would confirm though many were the chances she had to be otherwise looking after her figure as she did and though she didn't herself go to church she had been brought up in a good Christian home and had been compelled to attend Sunday School twice of a Sabbath and she had told Rodney that Jesus did not love him when he cut holes in even the Widmerpool jerseys no matter how they deserved it and would I please talk to Rodney about the demon Temper before it got him in its grip as he was a good boy at heart and never forgot her birthdays . . . She then burst into tears.

As I could hear shrieks of laughter and buckets banging in the toilets (uproar always seems attendant on the New Maths), I reluctantly did not contest the interesting theory that Jesus's love for Rodney would be diminished by this episode and asked her if she would mend the 2nd Widmerpool's jersey.

'Oh no,' she said. '*Definitely* not! I'll definitely not have *that* woman's foul garments in *my* house as it is definitely well known all over the Estate and my neighbour Mrs. Tusswell that they are carriers of lops and they say the Council definitely cleansed out her house with the gas. But, since that you are siding with their son against me and Rodney, he can have one of our old ones.'

Decided to ambush Rodney when next he is tempted to lay about him with fists, feet or handicraft-tool and, on the instant, chastise him, as it is well known in old-fashioned educational circles that the demon Temper is daunted thus.

MRS. WIDMERPOOL TO HARPOLE. (On back of pools envelope).

Dear Teacher you can send this damned thing back where it came from. Mr. Widmerpool brings home just as good money as her man and better as there is never no short-time down in the sewerage. They did not let kids cut up good things when that there Mister Chadband was gaffer of the school everybody is on about how it has got bad since he won the pools and went off with his fancy woman. Mr. Widmerpool is writing to the education about it

Yours and oblige Mrs. Widmerpool's sister.

If this is the end of the affair then Harpole has come off lightly.
Immediately Mrs. Cleethorpes began to enumerate the in-
adequacies of Mr. Cleethorpes it ought to have been apparent to
him that she was in a disturbed state (to use a current euphemism)
and could have been as violent as initially she was amenable.

But he showed a right attitude in inviting Mrs. Cleethorpes into
his office, and not as too many public servants do, dealing with
her summarily in a corridor. And again, he shows promising
tactical skill in putting a potentially violent parent into an easy
chair as it is much harder both emotionally and physically to rage
whilst seated in the new type chairs which automatically throw
the weight of the torso backwards.

EMMA FOXBERROW TO FELICITY FOXBERROW

Whilst having a quiet cup of tea with the staff, Mrs. Grindle-
Jones rounded on G. Harpole and almost shouted that the 2nd
biggest Widmerpool stank to high heaven and that it was dis-
graceful and that something should be done about it. 'When
you were an ordinary teacher like the rest of us,' she declared,
'you used to complain loud enough about the Mullets and anybody will bear me out this lot is ten times as rank. Well, now is
your big chance. Exclude the lot of them.' And when G.
Harpole did not immediately agree, she added, 'Don't you
support me, Mr. Pintle?'

'Yes,' said Pintle, 'I well remember my first Head, Mr. Amos
Treadwell, in Lancashire, and how he dealt with just such a lot.
They were called Samphire. He had the biggest Samphire out in
front of all the school after the morning hymn and caned him.
"Now you hulking lout," he told him, "Every time one of my
teachers gets even the faintest whiff of one of your five younger
brothers and sisters, be you personally as pure as driven snow,
I shall cane *you*." And years later, Mr. Treadwell told me this
same Samphire came back from the Army and told him it was
because of his school training that he had been made a sergeant-
major and that he personally had practised Mr. Treadwell's
method on dozens of acting lance-corporals i/c recruits with
similarly beneficial results.'

After play, I visited Mrs. Grindle-Jones' room and indeed
there was a rank smell coming from Reuben, in fact he definitely
tainted the air within three desks' space on all four sides of him.

HARPOLE TO MRS. WIDMERPOOL

My attention has been drawn to Reuben today. I am afraid that he had an unusual odour. I wonder if you would mind having a look at him as it may be that inadvertently he has soiled his underwear, which I am sure was beautifully clean when he left home. I am sure that I can rely on your co-operation.

MRS. WIDMERPOOL TO HARPOLE

My kids are as clean as anybody elses Rube has said as how that Miss Grinderjoan make him sit by hisself and the other kids take the piss out of him and twit him that he has the lops if there is any more about this me and Mr. Widmerpool are coming up.

Signed Mrs. Widmerpools sister.

NOTE FROM MRS. GRINDLE-JONES

I have had enough of this stench. From now on Reuben Widmerpool stays outside in the corridor.

JOURNAL

Went up the corridor and found the 2nd Widmerpool sitting at a desk and doing long multiplications. Told Mrs. Grindle-Jones that I was not sure that this was the best way of dealing with the problem as it might cause the boy shame. She hotly retorted, 'And it causes *me* nausea.'

Later in the day found Ringo Widmerpool outside Class 2 room and furiously asked Croser what he thought he was doing. He replied, 'Oh well, if Mrs. G-J. can get away with it, so can I.' I said (irrationally), 'Well you can't, so take him back, and the reason, if you want one, is that *I* said so.'

MR. BULL TO HARPOLE

Lucinda cried last night and said it was because she has to sit next to a boy called Ringo Widmerpool who she says smells and gives her a sick tummy. I know how kids get worked up, but our Lucinda is usually very sensible and I know how it is having been in the army five years and sleeping next to all sorts stinking something awful. I wish you could fix it that somebody else has their turn by him. And thanks for putting her up out of the Backwards she is a different kid her gran says.

JOURNAL

Visited Croser's class to give them mental arithmetic. If a correct answer was given the answerer moved up a place. Arranged four suitable questions for Lucinda Bull which put her beyond nose-shot of the 4th Widmerpool and three suitable questions for Vincent Slope and, when he arrived in the hot seat, I concluded the test.

HARPOLE TO TUSKER

All the Widmerpool children except Vanessa are absent from school. Can this be investigated please as I have reason for believing that they may not be ill.

OFFICIAL LOG BOOK

General attendance is very excellent but for the Widmerpools who are still absent. This is disheartening when they were making such good progress.

HARPOLE TO SCHOOL ATTENDANCE OFFICER

All the Widmerpools except Vanessa are absent. Would you mind calling to see them please.

SCHOOL ATTENDANCE OFFICER TO HARPOLE

I visited the Widmerpools to-day. They are all down with the influenza.

The Widmerpools are legitimately absent. The S.A.O. reports them as suffering from influenza.

ENDORSEMENT OF CIRCULAR BY MRS. GRINDLE-JONES

I don't know how the S.A.O. found *that* out because he was at Mr. Grindle-Jones' school at Sinderby-le-Marsh all morning and he went from there to our friend Miss Smethwick's school at Old Toll Bridge in the afternoon. *And* I saw 3 Widmerpools playing in a supermarket. If you ask me, he knows it's hopeless calling and invents excuses.

HARPOLE TO S.A.O.

One of my staff has seen the missing Widmerpools in a shop. As this seems to suggest they have made a rapid recovery, I wonder if you would mind calling on them again, please?

JOURNAL

The Attendance Officer called and told me the Widmerpools would be returning tomorrow. He seemed upset and said my second request implied that I doubted his first report. I warmly denied this, but he obviously derived malicious pleasure from reporting what (he claimed) Widmerpool had said. Which was:

> 'When I got the finnicky bugger's note I smelt my kids and they definitely were O.K. and you can tell that bugger we're not living in a bloody five-star hotel down here on the Sewerage.'

He also is alleged to have said that it was 'no use Miss "Grinder-jone" going on about his children leaving clods under their desks because if she could get from his home to "the * * * * * y school" without using a helicopter and not muck herself up, then she could have his "* * * * * y" pay packet next time they made him take a job.'

The 2nd 3rd and 4th Widmerpools are still absent.

EMMA FOXBERROW TO FELICITY FOXBERROW

. . . Vanessa Widmerpool told me proudly that they had *five* 'real' books in their house. 'Our Dad has two books, our Mum has one and our Kenny has two. One of our Dad's is a Wild Wester and the other one he won't let us see, our Mum's is a love story and our Kenny's is a war book and he can't understand the other and says it was a waste of money. My Mum only needs *one* because she takes so long reading it she keeps forgetting the start and my Dad only reads his Wester on Christmas Day till it puts him off to sleep.'

I later discovered that the book Kenny had bought with such high hopes is *Lady Chatterley's Lover*.

14

Mrs. Grindle-Jones is developing an obsession over the Widmer-pools. To-day in the staff-room she declared they should be 'exposed to the severest rigours of the Law', and (looking significantly at me), '*That* could begin with a prosecution for non-attendance.'

Miss Foxberrow, however, said that if Widmerpool did pay the fine his wretched family would get even less and cheaper food, and, if he didn't pay it, he would go to gaol, and that would stop their National Assistance.

She then declared that teachers should not 'pursue the ancient folly' of measuring up all and sundry against the respectability, rectitude and diligence which had advanced them-selves. 'If you really want to impress the Widmerpools with lower middle-class virtue, then give them a sight of strawberries and cream on your front lawn, Mrs. Grindle-Jones.'

Pintle then interposed, exclaiming angrily that the Widmer-pools and all like them should be sent to Labour Camps as they were millstones around ratepayers necks. To this Miss F. replied sensibly that there always had been Widmerpools and, if he didn't believe her, he should study his Chaucer and Shakespeare. And that layabouts abounded in Holy Writ. 'Anyway,' she said waxing eloquent, 'last night I saw Reuben Widmerpool wearing a pair of girl's red shoes, and this is an outrageous humiliation for a boy of his age, a horrifying and degrading sight in the midst of the prevailing prosperity.' She then went on to declare that M.P.s were too obsessed with Head and too little with Heart and would that Keir Hardie could rise from his grave and some of the so-called Socialist V.I.P.s sink into theirs.

Although a staunch Conservative, I found myself reluctantly moved by her words.

Hail Caledonia!
1986

A CAPITAL PLACE FOR A FLING!
North British Hotel, April-October 1986.
6 nights a week, excluding Monday.
£18.75—book now. Ring 031-556 2414.

Suggest to Smith g the only so old to the end

Reference the Widmerpools, I consider that the lack of adequate clothing and footwear may be a contributory cause of this family's poor attendance. I understand that those parents whose income is below a certain level can be given grants from the Education Committee Discretionary Fund. As Mr. Widmerpool, who is temporarily employed at the Council Sewage Works, only earns £13 per week basic plus family allowances, does he not qualify please?

OFFICIAL LOG BOOK

The three Widmerpools still absent.

JOURNAL

Mrs. Grindle-Jones in a very emotional state this morning. She stormed into my study and clapped down her register, hissing that 'Those Widmerpools are away again, every one of them. They get *free* meals, *free* clothes, *free* this and *free* that, family allowances, public assistance, subsidised rent – and they carry on as if they owed Society nothing. And the man has been sacked from the Sewage for idleness. It's a scandal.' Her eyes were brimming and her neck was a peculiar mottled red. She looked hostilely at me, implying I was to blame for both public dispensation and private ingratitude and declared that this 'affront to Society' would not be allowed in her husband's establishment.

At the time, I was in the middle of giving an infant the Schonell Diagnostic Reading Test. Despite the storm breaking around him, he went on stolidly reading, t-r-e-e . . . s-i-t . . . b-u-n – etcetera. Eventually he reached his limit at i-s-l-a-n-d, pronouncing it as it was spelled and looking baffled. 'Issland, i-s-s-l-a-n-d,' he kept repeating, as I explained to Mrs. Grindle-Jones that I also deplored the way the Widmerpools milked the State, and that I was continually reporting their absences to the Office. Eventually, as she still glared accusingly at me, I agreed to go round myself and see why they didn't turn up.

I may also have been influenced by the scripture which I read in the Morning Assembly, which was Isaiah VI:

'I heard a Voice saying, "Whom shall I send and who
will go for us?" Then said I, "Here am I; send me."'
Not that this didn't sound but faintly on my ears as I tapped
and Widmerpool himself opened the door, which led straight
into the scullery. There hairy Alfred, immersed in the washing,
seemed quite oblivious to all that transpired. At first, Widmerpool was taken aback but, being a campaigner on many a well-
fought field against Authority, he rallied and lied that, although
the children had besought him to be allowed to go to school, he
considered that their clothes would expose them to scorn and
was waiting for the Welfare to kit them. He then summoned
proof and all three absentees and three more still in the pipe-line
between 0 and $4\frac{1}{2}$ years, pattered in barefoot all looking very
bold. Nevertheless, I demanded why he personally didn't buy
his children clothes.

'You tell me where I get the money from, Smart Boy,' he said.
(He naturally has a T.V. from which to learn such repartee.) To
which (rather to my own surprise) I replied fiercely, 'Get out and
earn some!' 'Aha!' he answered, 'the Cruelty Man has just been
and *he* is a kind man who understands my problems and he is
going to bring the kids some clothes. So you can damned well
wait till he does and then I *might* let them come even though
they learns nothing.'

'Oh!' a voice behind me bellowed. 'So that's what you tell the
others is it, you hulking bag of piss and wind?' And it was the
Family-Care-Unit (which consists of Mr. Sykes the terror of the
district, and his glamorous blonde aide, Miss Chanterelle) who
had come up quietly behind us. This pair are rightly famous as
intrepid explorers of the undergrowth and waste-land of Society
and ambushed three or four lesser Widmerpools every day of
their working lives. He therefore walked straight through the
kitchen and into the sitting-room with Miss Chanterelle swaying
behind him on her very high heels. And, after inviting me to
follow him, he offered me (but not Widmerpool) a chair. In fact,
he instantly set about the latter in basic Anglo-Saxon, particularly hammering him for lying to me because 'my invaluable
assistant, Miss Chanterelle, whose only fault is her soft heart'
(favouring her with a lecherous leer) 'unloaded a heap of clothes
on you, you parasitic bastard, only one week ago, *and where
are they*? *Pawned*?' he roared.

Widmerpool absolutely quailed before him and the depressing

thought immediately struck me what a better headmaster Sykes would make than myself. 'Now,' he went on, 'here are two item of vital tidings for you, you lousy parasite, if you know what that means. And, if you don't, take it from me it's a b * * * * y insult' – (Miss Chanterelle tittered encouragingly). One – Get those blasted kids out of this house and into Mr. Harpole here's school. Two – With immense difficulty I've got you a job at Hobson's Coal Yard humping sacks, and it begins at one o'clock and I've instructed Hobson to hammer you till your teeth rattle if you don't get your back down to it. And told him I would personally swear in court that it was a lorry backing into you did it. And take your lustful eyes off Miss Chanterelle. We're not giving *that* away on the Welfare – yet.'

Widmerpool, now in a blind panic, agreed instantly to all this. 'I never had no chance,' he whined. 'Being put away when I was a nipper! I have been told my dad is a big Politician and my mum is a gipsy who wouldn't wed him and is now nobility. There is a man knows all the ins and outs of it and he is going to see I gets my Rights in the end.'

As we raised the siege, Sykes said, 'Don't mind my frequent use of the vernacular, Mr. Harpole. If I spoke any other way to such as him, they'd think I was as soft as all the other social workers. Now my assistant and I are going to lie in wait behind this privet hedge and slip back in three minutes to see what he's doing about it. It is what is known as "Attrition" and I am preparing a paper about it for our Annual Conference.'

OFFICIAL LOG BOOK

The three Widmerpool children returned at 11 o'clock this morning. I find it rather depressing that, where psychology and kindness failed, the outrageous bullying of Sykes succeeded.

I shall pass no opinion on Sykes' extraordinary visit except to suggest that those who train him would surely have been appalled at his brutal disregard of the gentle precepts with which they equipped him. Nevertheless, one cannot but be alarmed that he intends to announce his methods at a public conference since this will cause him to be pilloried by the Guardian. *The* New States-

man and B.B.C. T.V., lose him his job and thus make the world safer for loafers like Widmerpool.

HARPOLE TO EDITH WARDLE

My chain having come off several times on my way home I went round to the Police Station. The Sergeant looked furious when he saw who it was. 'If it's that spanner you've come about, it hasn't been handed in. And, if it is, you will be notified. There is no need to keep on calling as we have other and more important things to see to.' I said quite fiercely 'I don't think you have taken any steps to find my spanner, have you?' 'We are not in the habit of revealing the course of our Official Investigations,' he said. 'And now unless there is Something Else, I have my duties to attend to.'

We glared at each other and I should probably have left it at that had I not seen a gleam of triumph in his eye. As it was, I went straight home and wrote a stinker to his Inspector. I know now I shall never recover my moveable-spanner but writing the letter made me feel better and I enclose a copy.

HARPOLE TO THE INSPECTOR I/C
TAMPLING POLICE STATION

Sir,
For many years I have done my best to inculcate a respect for the Law in the pupils who have passed through my hands. Further to this, I personally have at all times upheld the Law and on several occasions have assisted the Police with information, considering this to be a citizen's duty. Yet, when *for the first time* I ask help from the police, what do I receive? I refer to the loss of my moveable-spanner. The attitude of your staff will not affect my respect for the Law, but you have my assurance that it has seriously impaired my confidence in its Guardians.

G. G. Harpole
(Captain T.A.)

JOURNAL

Having posted the letter wished devoutly that I could get it back. It is always a mistake to write in the heat of the moment. It is certain to put their backs up and they will now find excuses to persecute me. Bought a wireless licence and verified lighting-up times.

HARPOLE TO EDITH WARDLE

Returned home to find the house in a turmoil and Mrs. Teale in floods of tears. It appears that at about two in the afternoon a police inspector and a detective constable had arrived, first to examine the bathroom and geyser and then to closely question her concerning my moveable-spanner. Then, without giving me an opportunity to explain, Mrs. Teale went on to unfairly blame me, declaring that the neighbours were saying she was harbouring a Great Train Robber and that she was too upset to prepare my supper. To placate her, I agreed to visit the inspector and to tell him that I accepted the loss of my tool and to promise to take no further action. On arrival, a much shrunk sergeant obsequiously ushered me in to his Inspector who sprang to his feet and wrung my hands with 'Ah, *Captain* Harpole! How good of you to call and see us!' It was like Barlow and Z-cars.

It appears that all letters to local police stations are despatched unopened to the Chief Constable and, on reading mine and wringing an account of my previous visits from the Sergeant, that gentleman had given the Tampling area-superintendent a rocket of stupendous force which he at once redirected at the Tampling inspector who in turn released it with accumulated force at his underling sergeant. Thus my wish to have the affair forgotten was of no avail and it was quite plain that the recovery of my moveable-spanner was of immense concern to his advancement in the police service. On my way out I glared at the Sergeant who looked so stricken that I weakly felt sorry for him. Went home feeling depressed at my stupidity in pursuing the matter.

Like T. Fawcett, I must learn to temporize when confronted with injustice.

Last night I was invited to sing at the Business & Professional Women's Annual Dinner and obliged with 'Trade Winds', 'Sea Fever' and 'The Blind Ploughman'. These went down very well.

15

Pintle's turn for Morning Service. Hymns predictably were 'Work for the Night is Coming' and 'Trust and Obey'. Then he went off into a passionate tirade about a broken window in his allotment shed and how one's Sins would find one out and the Cleansing of conscience by confession. The malefactor inevitably sitting tight, he yelled for the 3rd Widmerpool to rise and confess. Two little girls began to sob gently and the 3rd Widmerpool, remaining admirably calm under bombardment, did *not* confess.

During playtime Croser predictably needled Pintle about it, saying modern kids no longer fell for such crude stuff. 'They simply don't dig you,' he said loftily.

'I don't expect to be dug,' Pintle says bad temperedly. 'I'm One of the Old School.' Then (considering rightly that this might arouse further derision) he adds 'And proud of it.'

'Ho!' says the Abominable Croser, plainly unimpressed. 'And what, pray, was The Old School, Mr. Pintle?'

'They were better men than you,' declares Pintle, rousing for the battle. 'Your lot are all wind and theory. *They* knew things. And taught them. *They* knew all the rivers that ran into all the seas. ('And all the tributaries of all those rivers,' murmurs Miss Tollemache, her eyes closed.) 'They knew every city and town, in what county or country it was in.' ('And what it was famous for: Sheffield for knives, Nottingham for lace,' Miss Tollemache contributes. 'And Epsom for salts,' guffaws Croser.) 'They knew everybody's dates, the kings of Israel and Judah in chronological order, the family tree of the Royal House of England, even who the daughters married. Could *you* inform us why, when the Stuart Line expired with Queen Anne, George I was invited to succeed?'

To my amazement Croser fell for this. 'Well,' he floundered
. . . 'Not offhand – but I knew once.'

'Just so!' said Pintle darkly, 'You knew *once. They* never
forget. And that's the difference in a nutshell between you and
The Old School.'

EMMA FOXBERROW TO FELICITY FOXBERROW

. . . roaring noise from Jas. Pintle's (One of the Old School!)
room, so went into my stockroom and pinned an ear to the
party-wall.

'IF I SAY IT IS WRONG IT IS WRONG,' Pintle is bellowing, plainly
beside himself with rage.

'But Sir,' some boy replies in calm and reasonable tones,
'I have gone through my working three times and carefully
checked each process . . .'

'BE STILL! I'LL HAVE NO MORE OF YOUR CONFOUNDED IMPER-
TINENCE. ANOTHER WORD AND BACK INTO THE CORRIDOR YOU
GO. IF I SAY IT IS WRONG, IT IS WRONG.' Silence . . . Mutiny
quelled.

Ten minutes, more cries of rage. Hurry back to pin ear.
Pintle bending slightly. 'MY ANSWER-BOOK SAYS IT IS WRONG.
SO IT IS WRONG. NO, YOU MUST *NOT* DO IT AGAIN. It is plain your
poor little brain cannot cope with it. Go on at No. 47.'

JOURNAL

. . . . found Titus Fawcett sitting in solitary state at a desk in the
upper corridor, looking surprisingly calm in mind. He acknow-
ledged my approach with a mild smile and continued working.

'What is all this argy-bargy about?' I demanded.

'Mr. Pintle and I had a disagreement,' he replied simply.

'Were you insolent to him?'

'No,' he replied. 'I merely disagreed with him over a mathematical solution.'

'And pray what does that mean if you would kindly deign to
use plain English?'

'He and I arrived at different answers to question No. 46 in
Down-to-Earth Problems for Eleven Plus Candidates, Book VI,'
he said.

'Well, what of it?'

'Mr. Pintle drew two thick red lines across my solution.'

'And why shouldn't he?'

'Because my answer was right.'

'If Mr. Pintle said it was wrong, then it must be wrong,' I said. 'You have too high an opinion of yourself, Mr. Clever.' Having said this, to avoid further discussion and show my disapproval, I turned on my heel and left.

JOURNAL

Found Fawcett in corridor reading a book. 'Oh,' I said, 'you here again! What have you been up to this time?'

'Mr. Pintle put me out,' he answered. 'It is No. 46 again.'

Not wishing to become involved further I picked up his book which was *Clutterbuck on Liberty* (Juvenile edition). 'And where did you get hold of this rubbish?' I remarked.

'Miss Foxberrow lent it me.'

'Oh,' I said. 'And do you understand it, pray?'

'In parts. But I disagree with some things.'

'Indeed!' I said.

'Yes – contrary to what this book says, I know that there are occasions when it must be enough to *know* one is *right* and to allow others who are *wrong* to also know they are *right*.'

'Have you discussed this interesting theory with Miss Foxberrow?' I asked with some interest.

'No,' he said. 'Miss Foxberrow is what Clutterbuck calls an "All-or-Nothing Incorruptible" and believes that Truth must always be made to triumph.'

Ascertaining Theaker was cleaning at the other end of the building, visited Pintle's room at 4.45 p.m. and examined the maths book they are working through. The problem appeared to be a quite simple one:

Whilst A erects 18 yards of a landowner's estate wall to a height of 9 feet per 12 hour day, his workmate B digs an adjacent drainage ditch $4\frac{1}{2}$ feet deep and 30 yards long per 10 hour day. C, however, dismantles 10 yards of this wall to a height of 3 feet and fills in 15 yards of ditch per 8 hour

94

night. If A and B began work on January 1st, 1916 and C began his 'work' on February 1st of the same year, at what time of day and what dates would:

(a) the wall of 2 miles 7 furs. 6 chns. 18 yds. and,
(b) the ditch one-tenth longer in circumference be completed?

Nevertheless, having spent a good half-hour trying vainly to solve it, I gave it up, thanking God for answer-books.

TITUS FAWCETT TO MESSRS. GRADGRIND,
EDUCATIONAL PUBLISHERS

In my opinion and in the opinion of another who does not wish his name to be mentioned, the answer to No. 46 in *Arithmetical Problems for Eleven Plus Candidates* Bk. VI should be*
whereas your answer book says it is 8 a.m., Dec. 18th 1916. Will you decide this please?

PERSONAL
CHAIRMAN OF MESSRS. GRADGRIND LTD. TO
TITUS FAWCETT

I have asked Mr. J. G. Jagger, the well-known compiler of school text books and author of our popular series, *Problems for Eleven Plus Candidates*, to look into your letter and he finds that there indeed has been a printer's error which passed unnoticed in proof-reading. Thus the solution propounded by you is correct. I am very grateful to you for drawing our attention to this and you may rest assured that it will be rectified in future editions.

You are a clever little chap and I enclose a Postal Order for 5/- with which to purchase bullseyes.

EMMA FOXBERROW TO FELICITY FOXBERROW

I am gratified by your interest in the Pintle/Titus confrontation

*The publishers have refused consent for the answer to be quoted since this text-book still sells steadily.

and can now retail the denouement since great emotional stress waves drew me to my listening-post only yestermorn in maths sets. It really was quite alarming, Pintle being quite incoherent, just making loud *roaring sounds*. Later I drew out the story from Titus and here it is ...

JOURNAL

Found Fawcett out in the corridor again.

'What!' I exclaimed. 'Has Mr. Pintle had to put you out again? You are going too far and I shall now punish you.'

'No,' he said, 'I left the room of my free will because my presence and a letter was causing Mr. Pintle such distress. But our differences are now settled and, when he has had time to reconsider, you will not find me out here again, Mr. Harpole.'

I am mystified by the entire business.

16

You are invited to attend an interview for the headship of
Ada Crescent J. School (Grp. VI) which will shortly become
vacant with the retirement of the Headmaster, Mr. H. S.
Stoneacre. This school has a long tradition of National Savings
and plain needlework, and the Managers have expressed a
desire that the successful candidate will continue this tradition.

Reasonable expenses and either bus or second-class rail fare
will be refunded.

STONEACRE TO HARPOLE, (duplicated)

I am given to understand that you have been put on a short-list
of three from which my successor will be chosen. It gives me
pleasure to invite you and the other two candidates to visit Ada
Crescent so that I can explain my methods, since on one of you
my mantle will fall.

EMMA FOXBERROW TO FELICITY FOXBERROW

. . . . Poor H(arpole) had an absolutely devastating do last week.
It upset him so much that he let it out (the bare bones anyway)
in the staffroom and I can piece together the rest. He had gone
to Melchester to see a school he's up for with two other candidates. It appears that it was in the Blackfen district, which is
where the gas works are, and everywhere not only smells and
looks alike, but sounds so, having been disfigured by some
builder who couldn't even think of names for the streets after
he'd built 'em. So they go in series like Ada Road, Ada Avenue,
Ada Terrace, Ada Place, Ada Grove and so on. Anyway, in

this brick maze, H. loses his way and gets off the bus at the wrong stop, runs around like mad and gets there late, in a great sweat, and finds nobody about. Eventually he penetrates the jungle of clothes pegs that screens the working parts of Victorian education factories, but when he reaches the Sanctum the door is shut. Yet he can hear a murmur of voices inside. He thinks, 'This is going to create a terrible impression of me. Being unpunctual. Mr. Stoneacre need only drop a word in the right place and I've had it.'

Anyway, he plucks up courage and taps gently. 'Go away!' a voice shouts from inside. So H. retreats into the pegs again and lurks, biting his nails with vexation but brings himself to the boil again by reflecting that the other two candidates are getting an unfair advantage of him – and taps again.

'GO AWAY!' bawls the Voice, 'I'M BUSY!'

By this time H. is in an awful state and would have caught a bus back to base but for the hope of preferment which lurks in every manly heart, so he screws up his courage and knocks quite firmly. The door is flung open and an impassioned headmaster repulses him, braying, 'ARE YOU DEAF? I'M BUSY' and slams the door. Poor H. nearly collapses with terror and mortification and no doubt leans panting on a clothes peg, before asking himself if he's really Harpole and this really is Ada Crescent because, over the headmaster's shoulder, he had glimpsed *three* backs already sitting dutifully round the desk.

Now you may think H. is a Big Joke and, once, I did myself, but lately I begin to perceive glimmers of spirit in the man (as you will see). With truly superhuman valour, he presents himself yet again at the breach, hammers violently and, when the door is flung open by the now demented headmaster, pushes in his big foot and shouts above the furious rebuttals, 'MY NAME IS GEORGE HARPOLE AND YOU INVITED ME HERE.' The headmaster gives back. 'You can't be,' he says, 'for there are *three* candidates here already.'

At this, one rises sheepishly to his feet and mutters guiltily that this was not true – he had been waiting outside with the two others, but really he was the new milkman coming for next week's order but 'once Mr. Stoneacre, Sir, you had begun to explain your System of Education, I didn't like to interrupt and I have gleaned much from it and in fact have resolved to put in for a Mature Persons' Teacher-Training Course.'

I was not successful at Melchester. Anyway, if it meant perpetuating Stoneacre's Primeval system, I'm not sorry. I hope the milkman gets the job.

Harpole is too easily discouraged. Although one would not wish him to lose his touching belief that Virtue triumphs in the end he must learn that not enough people with preferments in their pockets are capable of perceiving Virtue unless it is hung aloft like a flag and wagged before their noses.

HARPOLE TO EDITH WARDLE

A most extraordinary experience this morning, it being Miss Foxberrow's turn to take Morning Service. She told the children to keep their eyes open during her Prayer which she couched in casual language addressed to *Her*. One passage went something like this:

> 'And another thing we may as well ask Her whilst we are about it and that is that she will remind us to be kinder to one another. And, after that, to draw our attention to the fact that the colour of the skin of the Indian family which has moved into Railway Terrace has nothing to do with anything except oriental weather . . .'

As you can imagine, dearest, there was an awful row in the staff-room at playtime, Croser as usual at the bottom of it. When I quietly entered he was asking her, 'Do you not *believe*?'

'Believe in *what*?' Miss F. says (irritably).

'Believe in God, in *Him*?'

'No I don't,' she snaps.

'Don't you believe in anything then?'

'Yes,' she replies. 'I believe in the Holy Spirit which is in the hearts of most women and some men. Which is more than you do, Croser,' she added flatly and to my glee. 'You do not even believe the Mumbo Jumbo you rant on about. In fact, I doubt if you have even *thought* about it. As for the Holy Spirit He fled from your breast at the age of 5 years 3 months or

thereabouts. If ever I saw one more certainly en route to the
Everlasting Bonfire with its attendant Pit which is specially
reserved for slimy hypocrites, it is you.'

The bell then rang.

Croser looked properly crushed.

OFFICIAL LOG BOOK

Today held a staff meeting to arrange Sports Day. I expressed a
desire to be relieved from responsibility this year. After some
discussion it was decided that the most recently appointed
member of staff should undertake arrangements. Miss Foxberrow agreed to this with the proviso that the rest of us would
undertake whatever offices she allocated to us.

CIRCULAR TO ALL STAFF FROM MISS FOXBERROW

Initial arrangements for the Sports.

(i) Date – to be announced on the day itself in conjunction
with the weather forecast. There will be no individual prizes and
the competition will be between Houses. Each House will be in
charge of a teacher. General duties – Mr. Harpole. I will do
everything else.

JOURNAL

Words in the staffroom today, Pintle complaining that he
needed more details of Sports Day arrangements, particularly
the date. I also hinted at my worry. 'How can the parents attend
if they don't know until the dinner-time of the Day itself?'
asked Pintle.

'Surely you do not suppose that sports days are for parents?'
asked Miss Foxberrow, showing exaggerated incredulity. 'Am I
expected then to be arranging some demonstration? However,
if Mr. Pintle would like to take charge and run this thing to fit
his strongly held views I will step down with the greatest of
pleasure.'

Pintle immediately withdrew from his condemnatory position,

muttering that it was only a thought that had happened to cross his mind. 'Oh yes,' went on Miss Foxberrow, speaking with great determination. 'If I am to be in charge, then I assume that you all have faith in my competence. It is true that I have never before arranged a sports day but I have observed a number and, through suffering, have developed certain views about this ancient rite.'

As a compromise and to neutralize parental criticism, it was agreed that they should not be called The School Sports but Miss Foxberrow's Sports.

CIRCULAR FROM MISS FOXBERROW

Children,
At My Sports I want you to sit in your Houses around your House-teacher. This will be your Base and there will be a prize of a large cake given by Mr. Bull for the House that decorates the Base in the most exciting fashion. High marks will be given by me for bold placards declaring the House's confidence in defeating all other Houses. There will be no marks for modesty.

If you win one of my races you are asked not to keep the bag of sweets but to pour them into a House Pool for equal sharing when all is over. You will find that what you lose in sugar you will gain in popularity.

When it is known which House has won, it would be nice if that House carried its teacher around in triumph on a table so that other Houses might have opportunity to congratulate him or her.

NOTE FROM MRS. GRINDLE-JONES
TO MISS FOXBERROW

You can count me out from this ridiculous business.

MISS FOXBERROW TO MRS. GRINDLE-JONES

You agreed to co-operate if I took charge. I shall now assume that *you* are in charge. You can rely on *my* co-operation.

Well, if that is your attitude, I will do as you ask, but please remember that we are not all as young as we once were.

JOURNAL

Today turning out hot and calm, Miss Foxberrow said that her sports would begin at 2 p.m. and circulated a list of events specifying that, to prevent hogging by swift and dextrous children, no child could be entered for a second event until every other child had participated.

I was appointed scorer, Lucinda Bull's father came to work a Signal System which he had picked up in the Western Desert based on hoisting coloured discs which informed everyone which House led the field. I had taken it upon myself to invite Mr. Sykes and Miss Chanterelle to present the sweets and Mr. Fawcett had sent a very large trunk of pianola rolls which had been put out for the Council Tip and, to avoid giving offence, these were awarded as second prizes.

The course had been staked out in a ring and the Houses stationed at regular intervals around it. Miss Foxberrow was Starter, Course Steward and Judge, every event beginning and ending at her.

After the usual running races (which she explained had been put in to exhaust the professional competitors), there proceeded an extraordinary stream of events described from her cardboard megaphone as The Housemaid's Race, The Chariot Race, The Grand Boat Race, The Battle for the Bridge, etc., culminating amidst tremendous excitement with a Tug of War for which Miss Foxberrow had cleverly borrowed a building contractor's rope of such length that the entire House was able to pull on it. It must be admitted that there was much *joie de vivre* and, since it was to everyone's advantage for a prize to be won, the competitors' progress round the ring was pursued with deafening cries of inordinate praise or odium. Several times I observed Mr. Pintle to smile and Mr. Bull was frequently incapacitated from operating his Signal by laughter, he saying that it was 'better than the telly,' this being the highest praise known to him. I presented most of the rewards as Mr. Sykes said he wished to show Miss Chanterelle round the school and did not return for some considerable time.

Miss Tollemache's House won and to my amazement she allowed herself to be borne aloft on a chair, flushed with pleasure, bowing to the defeated Houses who, to their credit, cheered her loudly.

After every child had departed carrying its meed of sweets and pianola rolls, I congratulated Miss Foxberrow on the success of her Sports Day and expressed my disappointment that she would not be with us next summer to conduct a similar occasion. I then asked her what had motivated her in discarding the traditional Sports Day.

'Oh,' she said, 'they are so *dull*. Have you never observed the faces of those children compelled to watch or the meagre attendance when it is optional? Sports Days are for the fast, strong and successful and their over-proud parents. They should be held in private. Whereas the purpose of My Sports Day was the Pursuit of Joy.'

GEO. BLOW & SON, PLUMBERS, TO HARPOLE

I found this moveable-spanner in amongst my tool bag which it had got into by mistake and I am very sorry about the upset and trust you will accept this in the spirit it is sent in as mistakes can happen to anybody having a name for honesty as anybody can tell you and I hope the matter will be let drop now.

17

Strong drink is the Scourge of Society and never more than in this Permissive Age of Licentious Affluence. One of our panel of Temperance lecturers, Major R. S. T. Chivers, M.C., will be in this area on June 16th and I trust that you will wish me to arrange for our young people to have the benefit of his medical and moral advocacy contra the Devil and His Works.

Our lecturers are trained in the latest educational techniques and, although being equipped with expensive audio-visual apparatus, come *entirely Free of Charge*.

My daughter will be pleased to carry a verbal reply back to me.

JOURNAL

Decided that it would not be wise to refuse the temperance lecture since Alderman Tollemache has written personally, and it will give the staff a welcome free period.

OFFICIAL LOG BOOK

In view of beneficial effect on the children, I arranged for a lecturer on the deleterious effects of consumption of alcohol to be given by a trained lecturer, Major R. S. T. Chivers, M.C.

EMMA FOXBERROW TO FELICITY FOXBERROW

As a lecturer was visiting us, G. Harpole made a Never to be Repeated Offer of a free period to-day. God knows I could have done with it but decided I might be able to use the talk as a Centre of Interest. Although it was advertised as *The Evils of Drink*, if ever I saw a living and wheezing brewer's testimonial it was the Major, a lecherous and libidinous fellow who must have caused innumerable women to reach for communication cords. But more of *that* later.

'Well, children,' he began, *'They* have sent me here to turn you into little teetotallers.' He then went off into a maniacal laugh which lasted so long the kids joined in.

'Now,' he went on, 'we'll get *that* part over double-quick and jolly good luck to it.' He then produced an antique Gladstone Bag and peered into its depths. 'First I'll show you what *They've* given me to scare you with,' he said, gingerly fishing out two large sweet bottles. In one floated a small red cabbage whilst, in the other a wizened football had sunk to the bottom.

He then put on gold-rimmed half-spectacles and peered at the labels as though he had never seen them before. 'Ah!' he said, 'very interesting! *They* say (tapping the red cabbage jar) that this awful thing is the liver of a man of 80 years who never partook of anything but water, whilst *They* claim that this chewed-up bit of old boot is the liver of a sot who fell down dead in delirium tremens, aged 24!' He then shook both bottles as though mixing a cocktail so that their revolting contents bobbed up and down like bouncing balls, and everyone burst into peals of mad laughter (including Miss Tollemache).

'Let that be a warning to you,' he managed to get out, wagging a finger at us (renewed and prolonged screams of laughter). He then mercifully stowed the jars back into his bag.

'*Now*,' he said, becoming startlingly proper, 'I can tell you how I discovered the glorious specie *Crocus Oxusfilia* on the Steppes of Central Asia.

'With a party of sixteen native bearers I left Landi-Kotal at the northern extremity of the Khyber Pass on 15th August 1970 at precisely 6.15 a.m., dawn breaking in all its orient splendour over the Jahipura Range . . .'

Marvellous! Fascinating! Entrancing! Breathtaking! I'll tell you all about it in the hols. And, when you have passed 3 A Levels, *we too* will leave Landi-Kotal at precisely 6.15 a.m. (dawn just breaking in all its orient splendour over the Jahipura Range) to find a root of the glorious specie *Crocus Oxusfilia* for Daddy's rock garden . . .

Afterwards he came over to me and said, 'You're over-pretty a pussy to be an usher. I'm staying overnight in this hell-hole at The Fusilier. Meet me for a drink and I'll tell you things about India that Karma Sutra daren't put in writing.'

I think G. Harpole overheard this because he butted in and suggested I catch up with my class.

MARTHA FESTING, DAILY SCHOOL DIARY

To-day a man gave us a thrilling lecture on his search for the *Crocus Oxusfilia*, a rare plant only to be discovered in the Caves of the Assassins in remotest Turkestan near the source of the mighty Oxus river . . .

FREE WRITING BY TITUS FAWCETT

Men, I said, yonder lies the mighty range of Hindu Kush hitherto unscaled by human foot and beyond its snowy peaks rolls the Oxus River whose beginning no man has yet set eyes upon and in its verdant pastures the Sacred Crocus blows will you follow me thither? Yea sahib, yea yea the gallant band of Banjiis chorused . . .

SECRETARY, LEAGUE AGAINST STRONG DRINK, TO HARPOLE

Thank you for your Confidential Report on Major Chivers M.C. The Lecture appears to have been grossly unsuitable from one travelling under our aegis and my Committee tenders its regret for this most unfortunate occurrence. May I hasten to inform you that, although he has lectured to several schools yours is the only report we have received. Regrettably from chats with other lecturers on our panel, it appears to be quite common for school staffs to retire to their common rooms during these lectures and for the lecturer himself to be left as it were 'holding the baby'.

Please accept our assurance that we shall immediately remove this lecturer from under our aegis,

On questioning my daughter Martha, as I do daily, on what she had learnt at your school, I elicited the information that a visiting propagandist had impressed on her that alcoholic consumption is synonymous with sin. As my daughter is aware, I drink in moderation, my business commitments necessitating this.

I deeply resent this unpardonable trespass on my parental authority and, since you failed to satisfactorily explain the last incident involving this principle, I consider it to be no more than my duty as a citizen to report you to your superiors.

TUSKER TO HARPOLE

I have received a complaint from Mr. Alexander Festing of 'Tannochbrae', Plowman's Rise, alleging erosion of his parental authority on two recent occasions when scientific and, lately, moral instruction has been given. Please send me detailed reports on this including transcripts of all correspondence.

I am disturbed to learn that a lecturer not employed by the Local Education Authority has visited your school without prior authorization from me. This is most irregular and I must point out that the sole legal responsibility for any incident or accident arising from such unauthorized visits is yours.

A decreasing number of Anti-Drink lecturers, often recruited from superannuated headmasters, retired officers and failed actors gratifying their emotional need for dramatic performance to captive audiences, still roam the land. Major Chivers seems to have been an outstanding specimen of these nomads.

However, excessive boozing still causes much misery and shame, and it ought not to be unreasonable for a conscientious teacher now and then to draw these distressing results to the notice of his pupils. Teachers should not retreat from strongly held opinions.

JOURNAL

Visiting Miss Foxberrow's room noted a display of Child Art

purporting to be the *Crocus Oxusfilia*, the colour ranging from bright red to bright blue. An improvised dramatic play was also in progress in which Titus Fawcett purporting to be an explorer seeking the *Crocus Oxusfilia* was being attacked by a tribe of savages whilst scaling a mountain pass represented by the teacher's desk.

In Miss Tollemache's room the children were reciting in a chorus a poem retelling how a bricklayer fell off a high roof and lived, but next day, whilst drunk, rolled off a low bench and died. Although the Anti-Alcohol Lecture has brought me a parcel of administrative troubles, except for the two above instances it appears to have had no beneficial effect whatsoever apart from giving Mrs. Grindle-Jones, Pintle and Croser a free period.

18

Sir,

Through your columns it is my earnest desire to expose interference with ratepayers the circumstances being my neighbour
walking down the Tampling High Street and needing to
admonish her little son who is a good boy as I can vouch for.
Then this teacher from his school comes up and tells my neighbour who is well known in the district as a good wife and mother
that it is wrong to speak sharply to her little son and she must
not do so. This teacher I am assured has no children that has
been heard of and it is bad enough for ratepayers to be made to
pay for their everlasting holidays without being told off in front
of our own flesh and blood to wit our children and I would like
to know what the Council is doing about it.

Disgusted Ratepayer.

*The cadence of this prose is familiar. Have we not heard those
moral tones from Mrs. Tusswell? This is the sort of letter which
editors rejoice to receive during the dog days of summer before
garden fêtes and unseasonable floods mercifully assuage their
thirsts for tittle-tattle. It is sure to fire smouldering embers in the
breasts of dissatisfied consumers of education and provoke
acrimoniously rewarding entertainment for the rest of the district.*

LETTER TO THE *Sentinel*

Disgusted Ratepayer is right. My little grandson has been
turned out of his School Choir and has been crying ever since
and will not be comforted, his head teacher having told him he
is a groaner which is definitely not true as he has a sweet little
voice. The Council ought to stop it.

Old Age Pensioner.

My son was sent home by his headmaster last Friday for wearing jeans when his short trousers were in the wash. It is coming to it when parents are dictated to as to how to dress their children . . .

Another Disgusted Ratepayer.

Sir,

For two mornings this week my daughter has missed her free milk. Each time she has been told that there was not enough to go round. Seeing as we pay for it with our rates and that some others get it every morning that ever comes and never miss it . . .

Pro Bono Publico

Sir,

Pro Bono Publico is lucky. At our village school which I will not name (but everybody in the village knows which one I mean) it is my certain knowledge as soon as the school milk comes in the van it is taken over to the head-teacher's house on the other side of the yard and his wife skims off the cream for her own children who go to private school before sending it over for the ordinary children . . .

Only a Parent.

Sir,

What does *Pro Bono Publico* know about it I'd like to know? Unwanted immigrants want to keep their noses out of things. We English can manage our affairs without help from Iti's and the blacks. It wasn't us that had Mussolini.

Our teachers are alright. All my children got through to the Grammar School and my wife and I both take this opportunity to say 'Well done Teachers!'

Fair Play.

Sir,

Disgusted Ratepayer is an example of the uninformed parents which cause such discouragement to thousands of conscientious, underpaid teachers doing a job in well nigh impossible circumstances. D.R. would be better occupied urging her/his M.P. to insist on better pay for teachers.

Young Teacher.

The Vice Chairman of the Primary School Managers, Councillor Mrs. G. Blossom, has investigated the recent letter in the local newspaper the subject of which was a teacher interfering with parental correction and has discovered that the incident referred to concerns one of your staff, Miss E. Foxberrow, M.A. [Cantab.].

Kindly send me full details of the circumstances at once.

OURNAL

Asked Miss F. to see me after school and showed her the letter from the Office which did not appear to disturb her and, to my utter astonishment, she did not deny the allegation, even agreeing that, up to a point, it was true. 'I was going down the street to buy my weekly Ring of Confidence and a half dozen bottles of Double Diamond Which Works Wonders when I caught up with that awful Mrs. Cleethorpes. She was shouting at the odious Rodney who had jumped in a puddle and splashed her new P.V.C. tall boots. "I don't love you this morning," she was whining. "Nobody loves you!"

'So I tapped her on the shoulder and said politely that all children, even Rodney, needed constant assurance that they were warmly loved and that failure to do this resulted in them becoming unsatisfactory adults, incapable of warmth of feeling, generosity of spirit and undemanding love. And I added that even the lower animals knew this.'

I must have looked astonished at her candour because she said, 'Mr. Harpole, it is not enough that we teachers should confine education within the four walls of a building. We must be missionaries of the truth. Our influence must be a leavening in a world where brutish souls like the odious Mesdames Tusswell and Cleethorpes proliferate. Truth is Beauty, Beauty Truth, that is all we know on earth and all we need to know, as the poet says.'

'Well,' I said heatedly, 'that is all very well but I cannot put that in a report to Mr. Tusker because neither he nor Councillor Mrs. Blossom would understand or concur.'

'No,' she said, 'that I can see. In fact I am only telling you this

111

because I am beginning to perceive in you hitherto unsuspected qualities, and I feel it my duty to foster them so that my influence here will continue when my memory has departed like the dews of summer, fled like a hind to the mountains, as the poet also says.'

I said that I should not like her to think that we would forget her or that I personally intended to remain at Tampling for ever. 'Well,' she said cryptically, 'that only confirms what I have just said, Mr. H. And I know you will hit on the right riposte to this petty tyrant Tusker.'

HARPOLE TO TUSKER

Dear Mr. Tusker,
I have made enquiry into the incident you have drawn to my attention and, in my opinion, there are no grounds for believing that the facts given in the anonymous letter to the *Sentinel* are correct.

TUSKER TO HARPOLE

I do not regard your letter (undated) in any way as a satisfactory answer to the serious allegation Councillor Mrs. G. Blossom has drawn my attention to. Kindly let me have a detailed report by return of post.

Ending a sentence with a preposition suggests that Tusker dictated the letter under emotional stress. He neither can have expected nor liked this show of spirit.

JOURNAL

Seeing Shutlanger drinking morosely in The Fusilier I tried to obtain advice from him on Mr. Tusker's demands.

'You're too *close* to it,' he answered huffily and without appearing to give proper consideration to my dilemma. 'Things always go away.'

'But his letter,' I insisted. 'How shall I answer it?'

'Don't,' he said. '*Never* answer awkward letters. There's no law saying you have to.'

'But what will happen?' I asked.

'Why, for a fortnight he'll keep expecting a letter that never comes. Then he'll write you a furious letter and then he'll think if you didn't answer the last one, you're hardly likely to answer this and he'll tear it up. And he'll write something more conciliatory with a hint of reproach. Then you can reply vaguely that the Post Office didn't deliver the first letter. After that, you'll hear no more of the matter and honour will be satisfied.'

Whilst I was still thinking how unprofessional this course of inaction was, he began to tell me that his wife had asked him for a divorce so that she could regularize her position with the big lad from his Sixth Form. 'And listen to this,' he said, breathing rum on me. 'Do you know why she's discarded me? She says *he's* "better" for her as if men were vacuum cleaners. No! Never! (he exclaimed passionately). She can stay as she is – his b * * * * y concubine! And if I know 18½ year olds, that's how he'll treat her; *he'll* not help her with the washing up! No, not he!'

HARPOLE TO TUSKER

After careful thought I am afraid that I do not consider it within the terms of my appointment to make enquiries and written reports on colleagues because of anonymous letters published in a newspaper. I have every confidence in my staff and consider that to badger them on what they said or did not say, did or did not do out of school, would be to trespass on their professional integrity and Human Rights. I regret having to write thus but a point of principle is involved.

Good God! This is insurrection. Any hope of preferment still lingering in this new and embattled Harpole's breast must now have expired. He should now be looking around for such allies as he can muster.

But why should he regret giving Tusker this deservedly dusty answer?

113

19

This morning playtime Mr. Pintle insisted on my dealing with Matthew Jenkins, whose father works for the Gas Board and who had been grossly impertinent to him. It appears that Pintle (who was in a highly emotional state), holding his last ditch against the New Maths, had been following his System. This System is that, once you have 'painted a picture on a child's imagination,' he straightway will see a clear way to a solution. ('It is what I call the Moral-Dramatic Approach,' he said with modest pride.) The particular Problem in dispute concerned a householder, A, who, on February 20th, accepted delivery of coal shot through a man-hole which *exactly* half-filled his cellar (this having an exact capacity of five tons sixteen hundred-weight). Maintenance of two coal fires and a kitchen boiler required the maid, B, to descend into this cellar three times a day to fetch up 1 stone 2 lbs. precisely per trip, this being the capacity of A's scuttle. Pintle had required his class to work out the date when the cellar would be empty.

I saw at once that this was the good old hoary Leap Year catch, said so, and rose to hurry to the staff-room for my cup of tea before the women staff drained the pot. But Pintle was not to be shaken off. 'I painted the picture in their minds' eyes,' he said, 'of B going down daily after breakfast, on the first trip with her two scuttles and, on the second with one, following the precise routine day after day until the coal had all been consumed and A's cellar emptied. But, watching the children's faces, I could see that many did not fully comprehend . . . even when, using a wastebasket, I demonstrated by appearing and disappearing behind the blackboard to symbolize the cellar.'

He then admitted that, becoming exasperated at the children's stupidity, he had demanded if they had never watched their own mothers fetching up coal. Eventually one girl ventured to explain that they didn't have a cellar in their prefab, but she had read of them in stories about rich people. This encouraged the rest of the class to similar confession, and it turned out that none of them lived in a house with a cellar and that only one of them had even seen into a cellar. 'Never mind,' said Pintle, 'forget the cellar part of it. Imagine your mother fetching coal from wherever your father *does* keep it.' Then up jumps Mr. Clever Jenkins. 'Please sir, their da's don't burn coal any more,' he says.

'Oh,' I say. 'Then what do they use, pray?'

'Gas it is,' he says.

'Just because your father helps in the manufacture of gas,' I say, 'doesn't mean we must all use it.'

'All their mums go out to the work,' he replies cheekily. 'The new pattern of society it is, my da says. When they get back to their houses, it is warm they want them.'

'Rubbish!' I say.

'Ask them' he says. 'And you will see it is the truth I have been telling.'

'I'll do no such thing,' I tell him.

Then Pintle turned dramatically to me and said, 'He's waiting outside your office, and I shall expect him to be severely punished for insolence.'

Well, I was in a dilemma. This, by no means, was a straight-forward case of insubordination. On the other hand, I did not wish to give offence to Pintle, so I asked him if he would let me think about it. He then gave a derisory snort and said, 'Don't tell me. You're all the same – dodging your responsibilities. It's plain you won't back up the staff against the children.' And he rushed past me to the door. I am ashamed to say that at this point my patience deserted me and I leapt up too. 'Listen, Mr. Pintle,' I shouted. 'And come back here. You asked to see me, not me to see you. So now it's my turn.' That shook him to the core. 'Did you bother to check up if he was right?' I cried. 'No, I bet you didn't! The world's rolled on since you were a boy in Bayswater and it won't stop. Perhaps they *do* use gas. And I can't see where he was being cheeky. He was just saying what he believed to be true. Damn it, we're here to educate these kids to be free men *not* slaves. This is a school not a broiler-house.' He looked aghast and, when he saw I'd finished, scuttled off whilst I went to look for Matthew Jenkins, but he had tactfully disappeared too.

Well done Harpole! Why indeed should he bolster Pintle's in-
tolerance? If Pintle persists in using Victorian households as the
backcloth for his mathematical charades he has only himself to
blame for failure to communicate. Imagination boggles at the
plight of children tossed recklessly between Harpole's New Maths,
Miss Foxberrow's No Maths and Pintle's Medieval Maths! If
Harpole has anything on his conscience it must be his failure to
draw up a maths syllabus he believes in and then, for good or ill,
enforcing it. Nevertheless, in dramatizing problems Pintle is on
to a good thing so long as he keeps up with the current social
scene. When Harpole has cooled down he might suggest that
Pintle writes a monograph on his theory for the local university
Department of Education's quarterly where it will be taken up as
his own idea by some professor who will misuse his place on a
university press board to pad it up and publish it as his own, all
text-books (as is well known) being quarried from other text-
books.

JOURNAL

Somewhat ashamed at my ill-tempered outburst, Pintle being an
elderly man and probably embittered by being passed over for
promotion. Looked him up in his room after school and, making
no reference to our tiff, said how interesting and original I had
found his theory on Dramatizing Mathematical Problems.

'Oh,' he said, looking very chuff. 'As a matter of fact when
I was out in Meerschaum on the Deccan some forty years ago,
as tutor to the Maharajah's two legitimate sons, His Highness,
who often attended my morning lessons, explained that he did so
because my Moral Dramatizations shed so fascinating a light
on English Society. In fact, he urged me to write a little book
on my theory which he then paid to be printed and bound in
real skin. I will lend you a copy.'

20

. . . oh yes . . . going home latish I spied Fred Billitt, who I have
mentioned before, head-downwards in the playground wire
refuse container. I waited till he surfaced and asked him what
he was doing. 'Oh,' he said, with commendable presence of mind
and hiding discarded scraps of other kids' elevenses behind his
back, 'I was looking for a comic I lost.' Next day I had a good
look at him during assembly and then examined the other three
washed-out and hollow-eyed Billitts before telling G. Harpole
the family was undernourished.

'Undernourished!' he said. 'They can't be. Nobody's undernourished these days. They're just like that naturally. I've had
six through my hands and they all looked like that. It's in the
family on the mother's side.'

'How do you mean on the mother's side?' I asked. 'Why not
the father's side? Is it because he has to be fed like a turkey-cock
on the kids' family allowances while they watch him guzzle?
You should arrange for them to be medically examined for
starvation.'

'Oh no,' he protested. 'They would think I was mad at the
Medical if I asked for that. They know the Billitts as well as I
do. But I will ask the M.O. to have a look at them when he does
the annual inspection next October.'

Oh these damned officials. Aren't they too awful for words!

Ask Daddy if I can bring six Billitts home for a week in the
holidays. They can sleep in the attics . . .

JOURNAL

Emma Foxberrow went off the deep end about the Billitts, claim-
ing that the father is the only one that gets fed. 'I know these

miserable domestic tyrants,' she cried fiercely. 'If it's a choice between Best Steak for one or Scrag End for six, I know *Who* will get *What* . . .' She feels so deeply about things! If she goes on like this she will have a nervous breakdown. Feel disturbed.

HARPOLE TO DR. O. MCALPINE, SCHOOLS MEDICAL OFFICER

I wish to report that, in my opinion,

> Henrietta Billitt, aged 10
> Fred Billitt, aged 9
> Gary Billitt, aged 8
> Phyllis Billitt, aged 7,

are suffering from malnutrition and I should be grateful if they could be examined at your earliest convenience.

CHIEF MEDICAL OFFICER/p.p. G.S. TO HARPOLE

As you are aware, your school's next routine medical examination is scheduled for October 21st/22nd. Dr. McAlpine is heavily committed with duties devolving on him in his capacity as Tampling Rural District Council Medical Officer. Furthermore he is going on a course. In the meantime, may I suggest that you advise the parents to consult their own doctor.

JOURNAL

Told Miss F. it was impossible to arrange a medical for the Billitts.

'The only course McAlpine's likely to be on is the Golf Course,' she said, 'and between 2 and 4 in fair weather he can be found there. And on wet days he will be found propping the bar. I have seen him when I go with Edward Muttler.'

HARPOLE TO MCALPINE

I consider a medical examination of the Billitt family to be a matter of urgency. As you know far better than I, children's health fluctuates and cannot arrange itself to fit pre-arranged dates. I therefore should be obliged if you would examine these children and the responsibility thereafter will be yours.

CHIEF MEDICAL OFFICER TO HARPOLE

My attention has been drawn to your communication. I consider the tone of this communication unpleasant and have advised Dr. McAlpine to draw the attention of the local education officer to your breach of our professional etiquette.

TUSKER TO HARPOLE

The Chief Medical Officer has drawn my attention to a letter addressed by you to the local Medical Officer the tone of which is taken the strongest exception to by him.

. . . I concur entirely. It is not for you to question administrative decisions. In future please forward any communication you propose remitting to other departments of the County's Administration to this office for processing.

HARPOLE TO FRED SPINKS, LOCAL HON. SEC. MELCHESTER N.U.T. ASSOCIATION

Have a look at this, Fred. Does the Union think we ought to put up with this bullying?

SPINKS TO HARPOLE

Sounds all wrong but don't quote me. I'd let it ride if I was you. You've got to remember that he can snuff your chance of a headship in the County with a word in the *right* place and, as any confidential enquiries from Outside will go to him, it just needs him to breathe 'Trouble-maker' down the blower . . . Need I say more?

Anyway I'll forward your query to Mortlake, the Regional Officer and stir him off his backside.

CONFIDENTIAL

Dear Colleague,
Whilst deploring the attitude of your education officer, in my considered opinion you should do as he requests, such action as he requires from you being, in my opinion, within his legal rights and the terms of your contract.

Forgive the brevity of this communication but I must away on an Educational Cruise arranged by the Bahama Shipping Line so that I can report back on the value of cruises as educational media.

JOURNAL

Told Miss Foxberrow that I considered that I had done everything within my powers for the Billitts.

'Yes, I suppose it is all I could have expected from you,' she replied with asperity.

'What do you mean?' I said indignantly.

'Well, are you not one of the trusties given special privileges in return for conditioning England's youth for the Broiler House Society which is engulfing us? Personally it is my opinion that they should pay you a much bigger bribe, because the Broiler House Establishment of politicians, priests and newspaper publishers have very little left to do when such as you have finished the initial softening-up.

'They come to you free souls, with the dew of innocence in their eye, still trailing clouds of glory. And to you falls the monstrous task of making them *forget*. You are a monster!'

'I resent that,' I said hotly. 'As it happens, for a teacher, I am very fond of children!'

'I suppose you *do* do your dirty work in good faith,' she said with a scornful laugh, 'since it is the way you have been conditioned yourself. How can you know any better! Don't take it to heart; you are but one of thousands!'

Harpole rightly feels uneasy. After fifteen years knowing he is right, this distorted reflection of himself rightly gives him pause.

One's immortal soul should not be casually waved before one's nose by a colleague.

HARPOLE TO TUSKER

I regret that I am not receiving the co-operation I might have expected from an *education* officer. As I have already reported, the Billitt family, in my opinion, are undernourished. This is retarding their education.

I should have thought you might have insisted on the Medical Officer examining the children.

TUSKER TO HARPOLE

I take the strongest exception to the tone of your communication and herewith return it for your re-consideration.

JOURNAL

Somewhat uneasily gave Miss Foxberrow the gist of Mr. Tusker's communication. 'One of these days I shall hit on a way of dragging these *Education* Officers face to face with *Education*,' she said darkly.

EMMA FOXBERROW TO FELICITY FOXBERROW

Getting on the job early to clean out our fish tank found Phyllis Billitt shivering at the outside door, plainly having been turned out by the monster who lives with them. Quite hopelessly dressed in skimpy cotton cast-offs. Got it out of her that she'd had a 'piece' (of bread and scrape) and a cup of tea for breakfast. Was absolutely furious and presented her to G. Harpole when he bicycled up and demanded what he was going to do about it.

'I can write another letter,' he said helplessly.

JOURNAL

. . . I informed her that I would communicate again with the Office.

'Don't bother,' she said. 'It is time for *action*. Pray excuse me.'

She then took Phyllis's dirty hand saying, 'Come with me, dear.'

'Where are you going?' I asked, alarmed (knowing Emma Foxberrow).

'You will hear soon enough,' she said cryptically. 'But I will not personally tell you, so that you can claim you knew nothing: I would not have your precious promotion prospects damaged. There was a time when I thought there was hope for you but it is too late. You have been institutionalized.'

EMMA FOXBERROW TO FELICITY FOXBERROW (Cont.)

Croser arriving uncharacteristically early, I got him to drive Phyllis and myself to the education offices.

The sheep, Minchin, in the outer office bleated, 'What's this, What's this. No children allowed in *here*. *It's a rule*. If you want something you have to write' . . . and suchlike slogans as we tore past him into the tabernacle itself where Tusker, the top man, was leisurely slitting envelopes with a paper knife (inscribed 'A present from Aberystwyth').

'Behold! *A child*, Mr. Tusker!' I cried . . .

JOURNAL

Tusker has insisted on a medical for the Billitts.

Contrary to my natural inclinations, I am coming to admire Miss Foxberrow. She is so much bolder than the rest of us and not cowed by authority or the opinion of others. Most of us teachers, and me more than most, are apprehensive of giving offence to almost everybody except children. I personally am becoming appalled at the lick-spittle kow-towing way I have got into when, really, all Tusker can do to me is prevent my promotion. He can't *kill* me! In future, I shall try to force myself to outface him when I know I am in the right.

McAlpine, looking huffish, visited. 'What's all this Tusker tells me about malnutrition?' he snapped. 'Nobody's underfed these days. Overfed – yes. Underfed – no. And how does a layman know if anyone is suffering from malnutrition (even if it was possible these days)? Do you still want me to look at these kids?'

He then saw the Billitts one after another, each exposing a scraggy chest for him to prod as he asked how each was feeling. When the last had gone he said, 'Now are you satisfied? You heard what they said – that they felt fine. The little devils are fit as fleas' – turning a charm-beam on me.

'They're so thin, doctor,' I protested.

'Not thin – wiry!' he said. 'Pity more pampered brats aren't like 'em.' Then, as he edged towards the door, he told me about the hard life he had suffered as a 'wee laddie' on a Highland croft . . .

'Why are they so *pale*?' I said in the tone I felt Emma Foxberrow would have employed.

'Pale!' he cried. 'What other colour would they be in this damned climate? You're pale, I'm pale, we're all pale.'

'So they're perfectly fit and well-nourished?' I said. 'And Fred Billitt only climbed head first into the refuse-cage for adventure and Henrietta Billitt's two faints in P.E. were just the vapours? Well, I'll put what you say in my Official Log Book and, if one of them falls down dead, at least the coroner will know officially that it wasn't from starvation because *you* said so.'

'Oh,' he said (his charm-beam fading), 'if that's your attitude, I'll have a word with the Welfare Service and their private doctor about them.'

'And what will your word be?' I asked pointedly.

'That is against our Professional Medical Etiquette,' he said with obvious relish – and went.

HARPOLE TO MISS FOXBERROW

The Medical Officer has now seen the Billitts and passed them as 100% fit. I am afraid there is nothing more we can do about it. Thank you for your interest in this unfortunate family.

MISS FOXBERROW TO HARPOLE

Anyone but an idle toad like McAlpine can see that they need food. I hope that *you* are not going to let it drop. Why don't you go and tell that bully Billitt to feed his family!

After due consideration decided that it was not my business but the Health Department's to see Billitt.

Went to The Fusilier but did not enjoy my rum, it being at the back of my mind that my knowing Billitt has several times been prosecuted for assaulting the police and his neighbours may have influenced my decision.

EDITH WARDLE TO HARPOLE

It is no use, I shall have to tell you: I do not love you. Well I do and I don't. Or what I mean to say is that I love somebody else more. His name is Edwin and he is a Glowsheen rep. I have known him for more than a year as he calls at the Salon. I have kept it from you but for months he has been pestering me to marry him and now I have agreed: in fact we are doing it by Special Licence tomorrow. I hope that you are not hurt George but I don't think you will be. I am not really your type and to tell you the truth you are not really mine. I am sure you will soon find someone else. What about that school-ma'am you keep writing about? We have put down a deposit on a semi with very nice neighbours in a good class road in Manchester where his Selling-Base is and we have fully-furnished it. I suppose it will come out anyway so I might as well tell you I *had* to get married and I'm ever so happy now Edwin has stood by me. I hope they make you a headteacher soon. You deserve to be. I am glad to have known you, you are such a good, decent chap and I'm sorry I couldn't live up to you and wait . . .

JOURNAL

Feel terribly hurt and depressed. Yet I recognize that I am more to blame than her for keeping her waiting while I saved up for the down-payment on a house and for the furniture. Cannot write any more tonight.

OFFICIAL LOG BOOK

A parent, Mr. W. C. Billitt, visited the school without an express invitation to complain that his four children had been medically examined without his permission. After a difference of opinion he left.

. . . was receiving my weekly pittance of stock from a very cast-down G. Harpole when in bursts our local gorilla, *the* Billitt who starves his wife and kids and (whisper his terrified neighbours) drags them out of bed on Saturday nights when he gets back home from the boozer and (wife and all) thrashes them with his belt, threatening them with double encore if they breathe a word of it. When G. Harpole saw him he visibly blanched (to coin a phrase) and backed away, nevertheless putting himself in a state of preparedness . . .

'Now you look here you smug bugger!' Billitt bawls. 'I will show you how men like me who *work* for our living deal with bloody trouble-makers. A punch on the bloody nose is what you need and that you shall get. And when I have done you, I shall do her,' (glaring at me).

'I shall have you prosecuted,' G. Harpole says weakly. 'The Union has a solicitor . . !'

'There was a man last week in the *Mirror* who only got fined a fiver for having a smack,' shouted Billitt. 'And flattening your bloody nose is worth a fiver – Anyway, the Public Assistance will pay for it.'

Whereupon he swings a mighty haymaker at G. Harpole's head who, to my admiration, lowers same so his attacker deals the office wall a truly shattering blow (it shuddered but did not fall down). And, whilst he still roars with rage and pain, G.H. reaches for a cricket bat propped with suspicious readiness in a corner and smites Billitt a full-blooded pull to mid-wicket across the backside which causes him to sink to his knees clawing the air and looking absolutely stupefied.

'Now!' roars G.H. 'You Miserable Ape! That will teach you to come to *my* school threatening *my* staff you —— you small-time bone-headed bully!' By this time he was beside himself with *rage* and looking glorious to behold and actually swollen to double size as when he hit those thirty runs off one over.

He then seizes Billitt by the hair but (to my relief) drops the bat as I could foresee the nuisance of sweeping up what passes for brains in Billitt. He then deals him an almighty crack across

125

his face with the flat of his hand which levers him off the floor and then shoots him through the door with a very clever knee release. Billitt, grunting with terror, flees up the corridor with G.H. bellowing, 'And if I smell but a whiff of you in *my* school or find but a mark on one of your kids I will visit personally to chastise you on your own doorstep.'

A great hush had descended on the building and it was evident that all lessons had ceased and everyone was listening in petrified rapture. G.H. then turns towards me, his eyes positively *glittering* and hackles rampant (with me quite limp with adoration and the joyous expectation of being dragged off to his cave and debauched).

Then he comes all over depressingly correct, straightens his tie, smooths his hair, carefully replaces his weapon on the clothes pegs and blushes.

'I must apologize to you, Miss Foxberrow,' he says, 'for being compelled to witness such a deplorable scene. I am afraid that, regrettably, I was carried away by passion and, knowing my feelings towards Corporal Punishment, you must be thinking that I am a hypocrite. But I have had some domestic suffering caused by a man from Glowsheen and, in a sort of hallucination, I identified Billitt with this man. However, although I cannot expect to be believed, *do* believe that this was a temporary lapse only and never likely to recur. Please forgive me.'

'Mr. Harpole,' I say swooningly, 'I do, I do. You were . . . Magnificent!' He looks at me as though I had shot him. 'Really!' he says 'I wish that I could feel the same. I expect even now Billitt is showing his posterior to a doctor or a press photographer, whilst in transit to apply for legal aid at a solicitor's. But I expect your class is wondering where you are . . .'

I now begin to understand the significance those absurd lines by Sir H. Newbolt have for the poor fellow.

What can one say to this scene? Except perhaps to point out that it is in the great English tradition of the ultimate necessity of violence to secure justice.

JOURNAL

To my relief Henrietta Billitt turned up with ten cigarettes saying, 'The Dad has sent these and to thank you for all you have done for us and he is going to find a job and give our Mum regular money and we can go on the Outing and we are going to have fish and chips 3 and 4 times a week. And our Mum says to say, "On the QT that's the Stuff to give 'em and not to hold back from having another bash as that's the only sort of Marriage Guidance the Dad can understand." '

Last night at the Methodist Annual Knife & Fork Supper I rendered 'Trade Winds', Sea Fever' and 'Arm, Arm, ye Brave', and these went down very well considering their piano needs tuning.

21

No, I am *not* in love with George Harpole (you needn't call him Boss-man: it's passé). If my last letter was full of him (as you say but I really don't recall it) it is only because undreamed of virtue has emerged during his interregnum. I think his love-life has gone sour on him because he has been charging around like a maddened elephant. Billitt was the first to cross his path but two or three others have been trampled too. For instance, my door *happening* to be ajar I heard him going on at Mrs. G-J. in the corridor. 'Now,' he was saying furiously 'I've had enough of this. I want these children treated as children not as Victorian scullery maids. They are not here on sufferance to provide the Grindle-Jones's with a double pension – they are your raison d'être, between 9 and 4.'

'I've never been spoken to like this before in all my thirty years experience,' she wails.

'*You* have not had thirty years experience, Mrs. Grindle-Jones,' he says witheringly. '*You* have had one year's experience 30 times.'

JOURNAL

Visited Miss Tollemache's class and found Theaker there. She was saying, 'And, as a special treat, Mr. Theaker says we can do Cut Paper Work tomorrow.'

The Class, like performing seals, then chorused 'Thank you Mr. Theaker!' – that individual looked so insufferably like a Board of Guardians at a workhouse Christmas Dinner that I followed him outside and said, 'Look here – what is all this about you saying what the teachers and children can do or can't do? This is an educational institution not a rest-home for caretakers. Your job is to keep it warm, safe and clean.'

Theaker was utterly taken aback at this news and began to bluster.

'*And*,' I continued, 'I shall not expect to find a note on my desk tomorrow containing any sour afterthoughts that may have occurred to you.'

I then opened Miss Tollemache's door again and called in loudly, 'You may do Cut Paper Work twice a day for five days a week.'

LOG BOOK

I admonished Mr. Theaker, the caretaker, for interference in educational routine.

JOURNAL

I am almost myself again over Edith and her Glowsheen husband and now realize that my conduct over the last week has sunk far below the high standard a staff should expect from a headmaster.

Decided to apologize to Mrs. G-J., but not to Theaker, and definitely not to Billitt.

Making my usual inspection of the building before leaving, found Miss Foxberrow, her feet on her desk, her skirt well up her legs, leaning back smoking an untipped cigarette and staring at the ceiling. Feeling sorry for her because she looked so lonely, I entered and, ignoring her breach of No Smoking Outside The Staff-Room, remarked that she must find Tampling and District even with the sea so close very dull after Cambridge. 'Oh no!' she replied, not bothering to adjust her dress and posture. 'Au contraire, I find it quite fascinating, as I supposed it would be.'

'Well then,' I said, 'you have the advantage over me because I can put up with it only because Bruddersford Training College for Teachers conditioned its inmates to put up with almost anything. I should be extremely interested to know what you find of fascinating interest here.'

'Oh, the manifestations of the past,' she said. 'Time's monuments and so on . . . This district is particularly rich in architectural wonders and they are not worn away by being stared at

129

like Stratford-on-Avon, Westminster Abbey and Florence. They are the reason I took this temporary appointment and, each Saturday, I make excursions to examine them.'

After further conversation I asked if I might accompany her on the following Saturday (there being no cricket match), so that I could see for myself what I had been missing, and to this she readily agreed.

JOURNAL

For all she has been at Cambridge, Miss Foxberrow does not care at all for appearances. She met me at the bus station wearing a burberry with a great rent from one pocket to the hem and her shoes were not too clean. This is a great shame because she is extremely attractive, being well built and a natural blonde which is much rarer than you would think in these days of Glowsheen plastered on everything.

'Oh,' she said disconcertingly reading my thoughts, 'so you do not consider me in suitable gear,' (indicating her torn coat and knee-length red stockings). 'Well, I do not see why a woman should get herself up like a gilded dummy merely to tickle a man's jaded fancies. Garments are to keep out the weather. If your need is for girls all glitter and goldilocks perhaps you should look up a psychiatrist.'

Having travelled six miles by bus to Wimperly we struck out on foot for Ferry Farthingale which is in the sea-marshes, and Emma Foxberrow being no laggard we got there by ten-thirty. F.F. is a dump and badly looked-after except the cricket ground. I pointed this out to E.F., instantly regretting it because she remarked, 'Yes, but do you not observe that the pavilion is an old G.W.R. 1904 1st Class railway coach? Only its present bizarre use can have saved it from destruction. I don't doubt but that there is not another like it left in the country, and I shall approach the Barchester Industrial Archæology Club to get it out of the weather and inside a museum quick.'

The church was of staggering dimensions, having not only a tower but a steeple and inside were pews to seat two or three hundred worshippers. I remarked on this and asked how E.F. supposed so miserable a dump as F.F. raised the £.s.d. to erect it.

'Oh,' she said, 'you must get this one thing in your head rapidly, Mr. Harpole, if your studies of the Past are to be rewarding. And that thing is that the Middle Ages were not *us* in Fancy Dress. *Their* minds did not rattle along the same tram lines as our Broiler-House Society. To briefly answer your question – they believed in Hellfire and the Everlasting Pit and this is a great incentive to dip hands deep into pockets.'

She then pointed out an area of decomposed painting above the nave arcade. This showed 3 ancient lords in fine raiment parading in a field of lilies and the 3 same, naked (with even the hair around their parts scorched off) in a fiery furnace.

'Who ever did that?' I asked.

'We do not know,' E.F. said, 'and that is what charms me. That artist was a hero, Mr. H. He was preaching a Bloody Forecast of the Peasants' Revolt – probably having just got home from a John Ball teach-in. Can you not imagine the manorial labourers' poker faces at the next Mass as their eyes flickered across first his picture and then their betters' faces? Or the rage of the latter at not daring to outface Holy Writ by ordering its instant erasure? It's all tremendously exciting.'

'But surely you cannot believe in Hellfire?' I said.

'Certainly I do,' she declared, 'also in the Everlasting Pit. And I earnestly advise you do the same. Then, you can console yourself that whatever *they* can do to you, can't be as bad as *that* and this will nurture the disdain for Authority which all of us must cherish.'

She then climbed nimbly on to a pew top and invited me to join her so that I might observe more closely the axe and adze scars left by our Saxon forefathers on a big stone.

'Excitement is relative, Mr. H.' she said. 'A civilized person derives more sustenance from such a sight as this than the blood baths and gross sensuality dished up by X-films and foundering publishers.'

I was much moved by speculating on the strength of the men who wrestled this lot into the air. I could not be described as a weak man but these boulders daunted me and I had to admit that I didn't know how they did it.

'They had Faith,' E.F. said. 'And Love! *Amor Vincit Omnia*, Mr. H.!' And at the same time gave me a long look which I consider significant. She also paid me the compliment of not translating her words and I consider this significant also.

The vicar then entered (the creaking door giving us time to get off his pew). He was a chilly determined man with his hair carefully laid out and plastered down. He told us it was a very ancient building built by the Normans. 'Many generations of the faithful have worshipped in this hallowed place,' he said. I was impressed to learn that there was an underground passage leading from the church to the Hall a good half mile away and that it had been dug so that the Great Family who had adhered to the Old Faith might worship secretly at midnight. He showed us the stone in the chancel from which they used to emerge, though he himself had never been able to upend it.

When he had gone, E.F. said irreverently, 'If there is one thing I dread in a church, it is its vicar talking cock. It baffles me why they don't teach them some architecture in their theological colleges. No wonder they are more to be dreaded than the bicycle gangs, leaving as they have a trail of sanctified devastation across the buildings they are supposed to protect.

'His *secret* passage!' she cried scornfully. 'I have yet to know a church that didn't have a half-mile secret passage that everyone knew was there but no-one had actually seen but definitely knew someone who had. Even if there was one – which is impossible – how could it have been a secret? Nothing is secret in villages. Villagers poke out secrets; it is their pleasure and recreation and has been for a thousand years. And what did they do with the earth they excavated? Eat it?'

(E.F. disconcertingly holds strong views on almost everything.)

'Do you not feel any reverence at all for the clergy then?' I asked.

'No!' she replied. '*They* belong to a Dead Age. Let Britons, each snugly in his little nest-box, sink deeper into a slough of selfishness, whilst half the world starves in mind and body – and *they* will urge the three elderly ladies and the two choirboys to pray to a magic V.I.P. to take note and do what *he* thinks best. But let it be mooted that Methodist ministers be elected to *their* Club, *then* watch them bare their fangs, beat their breasts and load their black balls.

'No, they have dodged the awkward bits of Christ's teaching too often and so they have had their lot. The Great Debate of our Time wants no more from them than it wants from politicians and their mealy-mouthed lackeys.'

132

'I hope your views never reach the ears of the Chairman of our Managers, the Reverend Micheldever,' I said drily.

We had a delightful tea in The Crooked Billet in Massingham Peverell – laughing heartily at its reminder of our own reformed parent – for which she allowed me to pay. Then we wended our way home which I found oddly exciting – my sitting close to Miss F. on the bus I mean.

JOURNAL

Filled with enthusiasm for Things Past after Saturday and decided to make rubbings of every brass in the County if the necessary permission can be obtained. In the meantime visited Melchester and purchased five rolls of wallpaper looking like natural stones and, before going to bed, completely repapered my sitting-room to give it a medieval look. Mrs. Teale said it looks beautiful and romantic and asked me to do the staircase and bathroom also.

Next day Miss F., as promised, came to tea and immediately noticed my stone wallpaper, examining it with great attention. 'It is quite extraordinary,' she said. 'No other room known to me resembles it.' Then she looked closely at me as though seeing me for the first time.

After she had gone, recalling her praise, I sat back bathed in a glow of well-being. This later was followed by vague uneasiness.

EMMA FOXBERROW TO FELICITY FOXBERROW

George Harpole invited me to his home on the Midland prairies last weekend. Across three counties by train, then un-counted miles of bus. At last, even that stopped and we had to tramp the last two miles. And his folks' farm was half a mile down a cart track that wasn't in the two miles. When he was letting me through the last gate he asked if I'd mind calling him 'George' over the weekend, 'just for the look of the thing'.

Mrs. Harpole, who is quite elderly, referred to Mr. Harpole Senior as 'the Maister'. I got on excellently with 'the Maister' and we had long intimate chats whilst touring his foldyard to look at 't'beeasts'. About George of course.

133

'Oh it's all *there*, Ma'am,' he told me. 'All it just needs is bringing out again. It was the grammar school and college did for him. Before them he used to have opinions of his own and say them out aloud. *They* taught him that it's safer to swallow whatever medicine is pushed down your gullet.

'But he didn't used to be like that. When he was a little lad there wasn't a bolder. But it's still *there* in the bone and marrow and just needs ticing out.' He then glanced quizzically at me and said, 'And I reckon you're just the lass to tice it. I never was over-struck with that Edie.'

Mrs. Harpole gave me a dozen eggs, two jars of raspberry jam, a sponge sandwich-cake and a very long hand-knitted scarf (which I enclose) and wanted to know when I was coming again.

I had never heard of Edie before but when I asked George about her he said solemnly it was 'a closed chapter in his life'.

I then said, 'I have always wanted to ask you about that big medal hanging from your watch-chain. What did you win it for?'

'Oh,' he said, 'For Loving, of course.'

JOURNAL

Last night I was asked back to the Royal & Ancient Buffaloes monthly Smoker and obliged with 'Drink to me only', 'I passed by your Window' and was about to begin on 'Come into the Garden, Maud' when there were beery outcries for 'Trade Winds'. They are uncultivated brutes.

22

MRS. GRINDLE-JONES TO HARPOLE

This is to formally inform you that I have despatched a letter of resignation to the Education Office requesting that my contract be terminated as from Sept. 1st. On that date I shall have completed 30 years pensionable service and thereafter shall be eligible for pension at the age of sixty *in some years time*.

JOURNAL

Thanked Mrs. Grindle-Jones for her courtesy and for sending in her resignation in such good time so that an appointment can be made before the autumn term begins. She told me that her husband will be retiring in a year's time having completed forty years' service and that, since they will now have to move from the rented school-house, they have decided to buy a house near the Front at Cleethorpes, which they love, their summer holidays having been enjoyed there for the last twenty-five years.

TUSKER TO HARPOLE

I have to inform you that I have received applications from three candidates for the post which will become vacant at St. Nicholas C.E. School on September 1st occasioned by the resignation of Mrs. Grindle-Jones.

They are *Mrs. Sacha Bielby*, Married, Female, a mature student presently at London University Institute of Education.

Mrs. Caroline Dempsey, Married, Female, an experienced teacher whose husband has passed away and who wishes to return to teaching.

Edward Pont, Male, Unmarried, a student in his final year at Barchester Church of England College of Education.

In Mr. Chadband's absence, I was invited to attend the Managers' Meeting called to appoint assistant teachers for the next school year. Mr. Grindle-Jones and Miss Hope (Head-teacher of St. Matthias C.E. Primary) were present as there was a local applicant to be seen before *our* interview. This was Miss Penny, a big girl with an unusually round face and a dissatisfied expression on it. She claimed to be able to play the piano up to hymn-difficulty which made her a very desirable candidate.

The Reverend Micheldever introduced her, first indicating Miss Hope (this notorious oppressor of young teachers putting on an outrageous glare of amiability), saying who she was, and was beginning to similarly define Mr. Grindle-Jones when Jones said unctuously, 'Oh there is no need, Sir, to introduce us – Nettie and I are very old friends, she being one of my star pupils at Sinderby-le-Marsh and before she entered college to train for the Profession she taught and played the harmonium in my Sunday School.'

At this, Miss Hope looked greatly put-out realizing that the girl was already in Grindle-Jones's pocket. So, for differing reasons, neither had any questions to ask her, Grindle-Jones remarking avuncularly, 'Oh no questions: I know all about Nettie,' and Miss Hope just growling. Reverend Micheldever then moved on to the usual routine of asking the candidate if she had any 'little queries' before the Managers decided to which school she should be apportioned. Whereupon Miss Penny, with unparalleled nerve, fixed the Chairman with a basilisk stare and intoned a Prepared Statement, 'I want it definitely to be understood that in no circumstances will I accept an appointment at Sinderby-le-Marsh School.'

Grindle-Jones reeled like one struck by the lightning's flash, and indeed the whole tableful looked staggered (even Miss Hope, now left in indisputable possession). After the dauntless girl had departed, Grindle-Jones, still speechless and looking like Doom, was told he could remain whilst my three candidates were seen and could have which he fancied of the two un-successful ones.

I was prejudiced from the start against Mrs. Dempsey because I observed scurf on the shoulders of her black suit, regarding this as evidence of an untidy and sloppy attitude to work. Furthermore, when my turn came, she answered my questions in an off-hand manner and, when I pressed her more closely for her knowledge of the New Maths, she bridled. Somewhat roused, I asked her what happened when one of her three children aged 8, 6 and 5 was ill. 'I have a good *neighbour*,' she said, giving this an inflection as though I must be dim not to have known it. 'But suppose it is inconvenient for her,' I pressed her, 'for instance, if she is ill herself or is on holiday?' 'Then I suppose I should have to ask for a little time off myself,' she said huffily and broke out of her corner by turning her back on me and saying to the Chairman, 'Are all these questions necessary, Sir, when All the Papers state that Married Women are wanted back in the classrooms desperately? And besides I am a Widow and Tampling being so near the sea would be so good for my kiddies.' Thereupon a large tear rolled down her cheek. Everybody, except (surprisingly) Tusker and myself, was deeply moved and Grindle-Jones, to demonstrate his superior humanity, even went so far as to click his tongue.

When she was asked if she had any 'little queries' she put on a winning smile and said, 'Not reely Sir, but whilst I am in this delightful little town, I should like to know merely for Interest's sake if this possibly can be *the* Tampling of the famous Tampling Longlife Thread.' The result staggered me. Two Managers actually leapt to their feet and the others, flushed with local patriotism, all with one accord brayed that this *indeed* was that Tampling. I was greatly cast down because, by this patently cunning move, Mrs. Dempsey transferred some of the Managers' own self-esteem to her *scurvy* self.

On the other hand Mr. Pont, who was a very superior candidate, created a poor impression amongst all but myself. He had a manner of great self-assurance and his answers were so full and fluent that he plainly was antagonizing the Managers. Even Alderman Tollemache, rising like some antediluvian creature from the deep, failed to shake him with his usual, 'What about Percussion?' Whilst Pont did not exactly answer the unanswerable, he gave so strong an impression that he had, that the Alderman sank back into somnolence with an approving grunt.

Mrs. Sacha Bielby's entry caused a great stir. In fact, looking back, it is astonishing there was no burst of applause. She was like some great, glittering and exotic bird of paradise and, except for Councillor Mrs. Blossom, so fascinated the Managers that the formal questions were hurried through at breakneck speed so as to get at the vital matter of who she was. Even the Alderman forebore seeking this fascinating creature's opinion of Percussion.

'*Now*,' said the Revd. Micheldever with relish, 'I see that you are a Hungarian and have just obtained a teaching diploma to add to the Doctorate of Philosophy conferred on you by the University of Bratislava. Yes! Very Good! Splendid in fact! The illustrious University of Bratislava! Now Mr. Harpole here is concerned about a teacher's personal little brood, aren't you Mr. Harpole?' (Whereupon Mrs. Bielby tossed aside her blonde locks and turned a blinding smile on me, giving me the distinct impression that, if she was appointed, she would not object to extra-mural activities.) 'Have you any little ones, Mrs. Bielby?'

'One,' she said, volunteering no more information.

In fact, from this time on she played with her cards very close to her splendid chest.

'Oh, and how old is it?'

'Fifteen.'

'At the Grammar School?'

'No – she boards.'

'Ah, then there will be no difficulty, will there Mr. Harpole? Which school, Mrs. Bielby?'

'Roedean.'

'Roedean!' exclaimed the Chairman, his revoltingly sudden interest in Education thwarted by the candidate's release of only the exact minimum of information. But he rallied. 'I see that you have been married to Mr. Bielby for only a little over a year.'

'My fourth marriage,' she said.

'Bielby,' he said reflectively. 'Bielby is a well known name in Melchester. I know a number of Bielbys there. Now which Mr. Bielby would that be?'

'Herbert Bielby.'

'Ah, Herbert! Now let me see. Refresh my memory about Mr. Bielby.'

'He is employed by the County Council.'

'An architect? A solicitor?'

'No.'

138

'Then in which department?'

'Public Health.'

'Oh, a medical officer?'

'No.'

The Chairman was – and knew it – losing face by failing to satisfy the vulgar curiosity of his colleagues in this heady migrant who unaccountably had alighted in their drab backwoods. What passes for subtlety in him having failed, he fell back on native brutal inquisition. 'What *does* your husband do?' he said fiercely.

'He drives the sewage disposal tank,' she said.

She then turned towards me, smiled sympathetically and said, 'Quelles sauvages!'

Then she rose, saying disdainfully, 'I withdraw my application: I feel I should not fully savour Tampling society. Nor it, me!'

The unspeakable Widow Dempsey was, of course, appointed.

JOURNAL

Finding Shutlanger in The Fusilier far gone in rum, I told him about my failure to get the right candidate appointed. 'Don't bother me with your b * * * * * gripes,' he said, 'I have enough b * * * * * s of my own. All you can hope is that the Revd. won't b * * * * * well live for ever. He can't tell * * * e from head about good teaching, though his preaching is not half bad because whilst brooding over all the wickedness there is in the world, I've been doing a bit of sermon-sampling myself of late and went to one of his and can report he's not so dim as he damned well looks. Do you know what the old b * * * * r said? He leaned out over his b * * * * y pulpit and looked the lot of us b * * * * y well over. Then he said, 'To watch the way some bastards carry on you'd think the stupid * * * * * * thought there was no God! I tell you Harpole, the old b * * * * * had me thinking. And I've come to the conclusion he's b * * * * *-well right. The way some f * * * * * * *do* carry on, it's obvious they *don't* believe there is a God. That hulking lout who stole my wife. I can see it all now, the crafty looks he used to give me during my Morning Assembly Service. *He* b * * * * *-well didn't believe in God either, nor in eternal Damnation.'

139

He then relapsed into a morose rum-sodden silence and I managed to excuse myself, utterly revolted by his blasphemous profanity and foul language and resolved never to be seen in his company again.

JOURNAL

To-day, happening to see the Revd. Micheldever in the Library, I went up to him and told him that a man I knew, 'a notorious loose-liver', had been deeply moved by one of his sermons he had lately happened to hear.

'Oh,' he said, showing immediate lively interest. 'Oh did he! What did I say that so impressed him, Mr. Harpole? Give me his exact words.'

'He said that you leaned over your pulpit and said, "You'd suppose that from the way some people conduct their lives, they did not believe in the existence of a Loving God."'

'Really!' he exclaimed joyfully. 'How encouraging!' And, asking me to wait, he brought his wife over from the Romantic Fiction Section.

'Dear,' he said, 'Mr. Harpole has been telling *me* about what a non-church-goer, a well-known sinner in fact, told *him* about one of my sermons he dropped in on. Kindly tell my wife, Mr. Harpole, exactly what you told me.'

So I did, piling on the former depravity of my now redeemed informant. When I had finished, they thanked me effusively several times and went off beaming with pleasure.

I feel that Shutlanger unwittingly has improved my career prospects.

JOURNAL

In conversation with Emma Foxberrow I mentioned the pleasure I had given the Revd. Micheldever. To my astonishment, instead of being impressed by my friendly relationship with the Chairman, she accused me of bowdlerization and said I should have reported the exact words. 'It would have done the old humbug no harm at all to have heard his native tongue in common usage,' she said. 'He might have been encouraged to take a leaf from the book and preach future sermons in tap-room English. It would treble his box-office takings and sphere of influence within a month.'

A new child aged 10 was brought from Melchester J.B. School yesterday by his ma. They both were smartly dressed (the boy even wearing gloves) yet apprehensive. I was pleased to learn that his name was George also.

'He isn't a very good scholar I might as well tell you straight-away,' the mother said rather defiantly. 'He was in 3R at his last school; they don't call their forms A. B. C., they call them P. Q. R. so nobody knows which are the duffers.' The boy listened impassively to this.

My heart sank, knowing too well that children transferred from C streams are always miles behind the least accomplished children in our unstreamed classes. 'Well,' I said, 'We don't have streaming here now so he'll be in Class 4.'

I then gave him the Schonell Reading Test, which confirmed my fears, his reading-age being 7 years 4 months. 'Well,' I said putting on a semblance of cheeriness and examining his un-promising face, 'he looks a bright boy *who wants to get on*, so we'll soon alter that.'

I then gave her Book 4 of an Infant Reading Course and asked her to hear him read every evening and to mark his place on a card so that I could carry on next day and check him through it.

'Now,' I said, 'I am going to put you in Miss Foxberrow's class and she is a very good teacher who particularly likes boys and you will like it there.' Both mother and boy were looking considerably heartened by this time and, having shed his gloves and exchanged a furtive kiss, he went bravely into Class 4.

'Ah, *George*!' said Emma Foxberrow, '*that* is one of my favourite names. We are all pleased to have you with us, George, and, at playtime, two of my boys will show you where every-thing is. As it happens, I have a nice seat vacant this minute by the window.'

She then stood back and gazed carefully at him before adding (or quoting from the poets?)

> 'I think thou be-est an Easterling:
> The Holy Ghost it is with thee.'

As we went back down the corridor the mother said, 'Do you not believe in streaming then? The last headmaster told us it is

141

best for the children as they can all proceed at the speed best suited to them. Now we have long been doubtful of this as my husband keeps on about George being as bright as a button when he was a toddler. In fact, between you and me, he says, "If he's dull it's what *they*'ve done to him, that's made him dull." And he said he'd read in the *Daily Express* that a professor had discovered that schools are where they make children stupid.'

'Well, that is going too far,' I said. 'But in my belief, Streaming is a negation of opportunity and an affront to human dignity. When *you* first looked around for a husband, did you sport a label "I AM A C STREAMER" round your neck for all to see, or did you employ the old-fashioned way of courting in which a man gave you a run-out and made his own assessment of your suitability?'

'Definitely the latter,' she said, giving me a knowing look; 'after all, there is more than one thing that goes down well with a man . . .'

'Exactly,' I said.

'One last thing,' she said. 'What was that about the Holy Ghost?'

'It was a figure of speech,' I said.

'Well, as a matter of fact I think it was very clever of her,' the woman said, 'because George *was* born on an Easter Monday.'

Harpole does not appear to be a deep and critical thinker about education. He regrettably treads loyally the footprints of the founding fathers, making only minor diversions from their time-worn tracks.

Nevertheless, he appears to hold strongly to a belief in human dignity and his crude declarations of faith in this have a quite extraordinary effect. George's mother undoubtedly has gone away congratulating herself on her family's fortunate move to Tampling. And her belief in the magical powers of Miss Foxberrow will be as beneficial as that best healing qualification of doctors.

142

23

It is my intention to visit Tampling St. Nicholas on Monday for the purpose of carrying out a General Inspection. Please inform me if the school will be in session on that and the two subsequent days.

JOURNAL

At loss to account for the impending dreaded inspection as it must be most unusual for a school to be inspected during the headmaster's absence.

CIRCULAR TO STAFF

There is to be a General Inspection by Her Majesty's Inspectors. May I urge that all books are marked up to date, that examples of the children's *best* work are readily available, most of it pinned to the walls, that the children be warned about their deportment in and out of the classroom and that nobody is allowed to 'leave the room' during those three days. The bell must be rung a minute or two later for playtime going-out and two or three minutes earlier for coming-in. Have a ready supply of pencils sharpened so that nobody is left without one. *On no account argue with the Inspectors but agree enthusiastically and without demur, declaring that any suggestions they make are excellent and will be put into operation immediately.*

CROSER TO HARPOLE

Can I have 4 doz. new English exercise books and 4 doz. new maths exercise books.

JOURNAL

On this day of all days, Emma Foxberrow had not arrived at a quarter-to-nine, so rang her lodgings. To my surprise she answered the telephone and said that I was not to panic because she was just setting off having forgotten to wind up her alarm clock because 'she thought today was going to be a Saturday'.

Harassing in-extremis day. Two inspectors came, a tall man who moved at a sort of run and a woman with an immense bust who cruised around the school like a fully rigged ship.

They appeared annoyed to find I was only temporarily in charge. The lady H.M.I. said, 'But Mr. Chadband particularly asked us to delay the inspection until this term. However, we cannot waste our time: now we are here we must inspect you.'

In the first hour, I received disquieting reports of their presence in Theaker's boiler house, the junior girls' toilets, Miss Tollemache's scripture lesson, having their weights recorded by a New Maths Group who fell to giggling when they couldn't find enough weights for the Lady Inspector, and going through Miss Foxberrow's album of Child Art with doomlike faces.

These alarms and excursions continued all day. At 4.30 p.m. a staff meeting gathered without being called, the teachers seeming just to 'come together'. (As Miss Tollemache said dreamily, 'Like the apostles on that first Whit Sunday when the Holy Spirit came down like Tongues of Fire.')

'Yes,' said Mrs. Grindle-Jones crossly. 'They come and what *do* they find? One thing they *don't* find and that is Chadband. Why should he be banging away at Bognor while we are sweating blood trying to paste up cracks in his school.' Whilst silently agreeing with her, I put my foot down firmly and said, 'Come, let us not be down-hearted. Mr. Chadband may be absent, but *I* am here.' (Whereupon Croser sniggered.) 'Well,' went on Mrs. Grindle-Jones, 'we'll know soon enough what they are *writing* in those little black notebooks they keep pulling out.' We were gloomily acknowledging the truth of this when E.F. came running round the corner. 'Oh, am I late?' she said. 'What am I late for?' 'What did they say to *you*?' we all cried.

'Oh,' she said. 'I have been haunted by That Man. He has been in and out all day blowing his nose because I think he has a cold. Then, when I'd set my children going on *What I saw last night in the rec.*, I went into my store-room to have a quick read at King Alfred on whom I was to deliver a homily when, to my alarm, I find *him* at my heels and the first thing I think of is that he has been waiting his chance all day and now is going to make a grab at me. So I turn to defend myself and find him not looking as peeved as you do Mr. Harpole when you see the mess in my store-room. Instead he pushes past me, cooing ecstatically, "Why! Why, what is this! What is this! This is like Old Times." And he prises out my ukulele from under a pile of debris and begins to strum it and sing in antique style, "Lulu is my gal, Who? Who? Lu-lu!" which I think was top of the pops in 1899.'

When we heard this, we all felt cheered because it appeared to demonstrate that he was a human being like the rest of us.

Then we all went home.

All evening have to stop myself humming 'Lulu is my girl.
Who? Who?
Lu-lu!'

Later in the evening I thought how unlike Mr. Chadband it was to forget that he would not be present when he asked for the inspection to be delayed.

REPORT TO THE MANAGERS AND EDUCATION
COMMITTEE ON TAMPLING ST. NICHOLAS
PRIMARY (J)

CONFIDENTIAL

Tampling St. Nicholas C.E. (Aided) Primary (J) Group 2, stands on a site of 1,624 square yards on the northern outskirts of that town. Although built in 1883, the buildings are structurally sound. Flushed toilets replaced earth closets in 1962 and three wash-basins were installed in the porch which serves as a cloak-room for the outdoor garments of the children. Two chains and plugs were missing from these and the overflow of one was blocked with soap. The premises are clean and reflect credit on the caretaker, Mr. E. Theaker. We recommend that he should be provided with a small room for his essential clerical work.

Miss Tollemache

There is much evidence here of conscientious hard work but of some confusion of aims. This teacher was a pupil, then a pupil-teacher, and now is a teacher at the school and inevitable vestiges of a much earlier era in education cling to her. For example, the class has been trained to whisper thanks in concert whenever the teacher opens a window. This we consider is not in accordance with the best educational practice.

In mathematics, it is recommended that this teacher should now fit in with the Common Market and United Europe by no longer insisting on the memorization of the more archaic land measurements such as roods, poles and perches. This teacher should be encouraged to be more adventurous in the development of her own ideas.

Mr. Jas. Pintle

Mr. Pintle, who is nearing the close of his career, spent the earlier span of it as a tutor to native royalty in the Indian Empire. He perhaps tends to give over-emphasis to discipline but the work of his class is dedicated and purposeful. It is recommended that Mr. Pintle be encouraged to attend a short crash-course on the New Maths.

Mr. Croser

Has almost completed his probationary year. This young teacher exerts notable moral influence on his children. We were particularly impressed by his religious instruction on The Child Samuel and the well-corrected exercise books.

Mrs. Grindle-Jones

This mature teacher is immensely industrious and expects the highest standards of attainment from her class. She is retiring at the end of this term.

Miss Foxberrow

This energetic young teacher is a Cambridge graduate appointed for one term during the absence of the headmaster. She has had some experience in the well known 'progressive' residential school, Winterhills. The work of her class is refreshingly lively. We were particularly impressed by her Child-Art, the readiness and ease of the children's oral communication and atmosphere

146

of happy community. We were interested in but did not entirely agree with this teacher's ideas on the development of individualism which we feel could well be left to the penultimate stages of education.

General Report
Despite disadvantages of an old building and a cramped recreational area, this school is fulfilling a useful purpose. *Esprit-de-corps* is high, the children are cheerful, well-mannered and lively. There is much evidence of progressive ideas being put to the test and a commendable absence of chilling authoritarianism. Opportunities are provided for at least some of the children to develop their individualities. We feel a great deal of the credit for this satisfactory state is due to the leadership of the teacher-in-charge, Mr. G. Harpole, who has tackled his responsibilities with liveliness and determination. We were considerably impressed by this school.

JOURNAL

Gave a copy of the personal reports to each of the staff and called a formal staff meeting to read aloud the General Report. However, when it came to the point, omitted reading Sentence 5.

This report is Harpole's passport to Preferment. One assumes that he immediately will duplicate a gross copies for attachment to future application forms. Although he might be tempted to paint the lily with mild, harmless editing (e.g. insertion of 'entirely' between 'is' and 'due' and the deletion of 'a great deal of'), this should be resisted even when faced by competition from rival candidates' forged or embellished testimonials.

It would be illuminating to have had a record of the encounter between the inspector and Theaker when the latter achieved his aim to become an administrator.

EMMA FOXBERROW TO FELICITY FOXBERROW

It seems Tollemache's pa, the Alderman, receives an official copy of our Report so she has seen what has been written about everyone else. 'They thought you were Wonderful, dear,' she said. It appears G. Harpole modestly omitted to read the passage concerning himself. I have rectified this by duplicating and distributing the full text to ensure the Grindle-Jones's choke as they lap their bedtime cocoa. Tollemache herself is responding wonderfully to the H.M.I's invitation to libertarianism. The old Tollemache holding wakes over registers and dusting wreaths is cast off and a Liberated Woman risen like a glorious Phoenix. Today in Assembly she taught the kids a new hymn with only one verse:

> 'Zaccheus was a little tiny man
> A tiny little man was he:
> He climbed up into a sycamore tree
> So Jesus he might see.
> And when the Teacher came that way
> He waved up into that tree
> And shouted "Hi! Zaccheus, come on down –
> I'm a-coming to your house for tea." '

All of which was sung-acted en masse – everybody sinking to dwarf stature before pretending to shin up a tree . . . and so on. Much merriment.

JOURNAL

Congratulated Miss Tollemache on her lively hymn-singing.

'Oh,' she said, 'I *do* occasionally have an idea in my head, Mr. Harpole, but I have learnt to leave it there for the sake of peace and quiet in the school. And one such idea which has been in my head for close on forty years is that I have never seen anything in a school hymn-book that children really *want* to sing.' She then lent me a copy of Sankey & Moody's Revivalist Choruses, saying 'Why don't you let us sing these in morning assemblies? If the children must sing gibberish they at least might as well sing it to a merry tune and the repeated choruses will be a boon to the slow readers who didn't pick it up first time.'

Decided to do this and duplicated a selection.

Halfway through our new-style Morning Assembly when the Chairman of the Joint Managers, Revd. Micheldever, entered. As we were already fully launched (with triangles and tambourines) on 'The Sweet By and By' it was too late to switch and to my annoyance an over-zealous child immediately handed him the New Sheet and pointed out the place. To my astonishment, he began to roar in a rich rolling bass, joining Croser and myself in the echo for lower registers which comes in the chorus:

'In the sweet By and By (By and By),
We shall meet on that Beautiful Shore (Beautiful Shore).'

Afterwards, he indicated how much he savoured a good sing. When I ventured a hint that I had supposed revivalist hymns might not find favour with him, being C. of E., he said, 'Mr. Harpole, my father and his father before him were powerful Primitive Methodist local preachers and "Sweet By and By" was my dear old mother's favourite hymn which I sang at her knee, and I should have been a Methodist minister myself but, as is not generally known, they have a barbaric custom of moving on their underpaid clergy every third year into inconvenient manses where heavy Victorian furniture is permanently installed to save expense in flitting. Whereas, once you are in a C. of E. billet, you are there for life if it suits you.

'But many's the time, as we drone through Hymns A. & M., I long for those fine old rousers, "Hold the Fort", "Count your Many Blessings", "Pull for the Shore, Sailor" and "We are Out on the Ocean Sailing".'

Heard in roundabout way that there was an awful fuss at the Grammar School Speech-Day – the Big Sixth Former turned up to receive his A-Level Certificates driving Shutlanger's red Triumph Sports (which his wife took when she fled) and leading in triumph Mrs. Shutlanger dolled-up in fun-fur over a microskirt and transmuted into a silver blonde. They took prominent seats in the middle of the hall, parents on each side edging away in horror because of all the staring.

Shutlanger himself read his report at breakneck speed, plainly wracked by powerful emotions. The Guest of Honour, Sir Frederick Wheeler the industrialist, was naturally unaware of this drama and, when the Big Sixth Former arrived on the platform amidst thunderous and prolonged cheering from the boys, he wrung his hand and is said to have urged him 'to press forward more strongly than ever, my boy'.

The two fugitives then left the hall, bringing the proceedings to a halt, but, by the time the third actor in this cause-célèbre had managed to extricate himself from the platform party, both his car and wife had fled again.

24

Councillor Mrs. Blossom visited this afternoon. She was wearing a large angora coat and a blonde wig, her hair being grey when I saw her last. She said that she felt sure that I had all under control so she would just sign the log-book, which she did – 'Councillor Mrs. Wm. Blossom.' Then she said, 'Why do we stay sitting on these hard chairs? Let us sit on the nice easy ones in your little corner'. When we had done so, she pulled up her chair so that her knees were rubbing mine until I edged back my chair. Then, instead of discussing the school, she began to talk about herself and how lonely she was and how she had never had what she kept calling a 'proper life' because her husband was 'that old and always had been since he trapped me like the silly girl I was'.

I prudently did not comment on this but made non-committal murmurs.

'Mr. Blossom is no use to me,' she said. 'He is hopeless and it will be a blessing when he continues his rest elsewhere. He is absolutely no consolation to me in bed nor ever has been. Even in his early fifties he fell asleep the minute he hit the sack. And nothing I could do ever roused him. I sent for some Congo tablets I saw about in a Sunday paper and crushed them in his cocoa but all they did was to send him tottering off to the toilet with the gripes and give him dreadful nightmares which made him shout and scream that the Russians were coming. I bet *you* are different,' she went on. 'You would more likely need a pepper-pot to fight you off than a pill to turn you on. It is all round my Ward how you half-killed that dreadful Billitt and it gives me one big thrill.'

Whilst I was hearing these extraordinary indiscretions with growing panic, she was hutching-up closer and closer and eventually put both hands on my knees. As I was too embarrassed to look her in the face, I found myself marvelling at the number of expensive rings she was wearing but she must have thought it was her red nails I was looking at, because she said, 'My toes are painted as well. Would you like to see them? Because I will show you them when you come round to see me. I like big men. Mr. Blossom is a small man and, Mr. Harpole, I'm a woman who needs to be managed. That's funny, as I'm a Manager, whereas what I need is a firm headmaster.' She then giggled, which alarmed me yet more.

It is very easy to slide chairs on Theaker's floors and this she did until her round shiny knees were pressing mine again and, because of the wall, I could get no further back.

'Oh, I feel just like a silly girl again this p.m.,' she said. 'How is it you are not married yet, Mr. Harpole? I know – you have a little chick somewhere. Don't deny it because I won't believe it.' She went gabbling on and all the time she was getting redder in the face, her eyes having a glazed look. 'You could have a flat at my great empty place and it would be at a nominal rent. Shall we say five bob the week? Or the month for all I care.'

The next minute she was crawling up me, having one arm round my neck and her face pushed up at mine, trying to lick me. In fact, had she not kept repeating 'Love me! Love me!' I should have thought she was attacking me.

Well, this was the last straw, and I managed to struggle to my feet and straighten my back, raising her up like a drowning person and, after hanging awhile, she lost her grip and slid off to the floor and got caught up in her fur coat. 'You will have to excuse me now, Councillor Blossom,' I said, 'as I have a class waiting. Let us forget what has happened; you can absolutely rely on me not to breathe a word of it.' Then I hurried off.

When I returned in half an hour she had gone. I am very worried about the consequences. Between them, Councillor Mrs. Blossom and Tusker will not be satisfied now till I have lost my job.

EMMA FOXBERROW TO FELICITY FOXBERROW

I have some astonishing news for you. George Harpole will be asking me to be his bride quite soon. I shall be bearing him home in Triumph for your close inspection in the holidays.

You are requested to attend a special meeting of the Primary School Managers on July 4th.

JOURNAL

I was kept waiting in the corridor for 35 minutes past the notified time whilst they were talking me over. Then Minchin, the clerk, let me in (avoiding my eyes). The Revd. Micheldever looked uncomfortable, Tusker simulated interest in my service book, Alderman Tollemache's head sagged but he was breathing. But Councillor Mrs. Blossom glared at me with hot and angry eyes. I said, 'Good evening.'

There was a longish silence. But, at last, the Revd. Micheldever said, 'Ah! Well I think we all are here. No-one else still to come? No? In that case perhaps should we begin. . .?' Then there was another silence.

'There has been a complaint, Mr. Harpole,' he said in the end. 'And the Managers have invited you here to help us. We want you to understand that we are satisfied with your general running of the school, the academic progress and so on. But there has been a serious allegation of deterioration in the school's moral tone. Perhaps you would like to read this.' And he passed down the table a page torn from an exercise book: it was soiled from being in a child's pocket.

'One of the ratepayers in Councillor Mrs. Blossom's Ward took it round to her.' He consulted Mr. Tusker. 'A Mrs. Cleethorpes found it in the jacket pocket of her child, Rodney.'

It said:

> 'ANTI-GOD CLUB.
> There will be a meeting
> at 7 tonight in the Usual
> Place.
>   Titus Fawcett,
>   Grand Master.'

'And,' Councillor Blossom hissed, 'it's no use to tear it up as I have made a copy. *This* is what things have come to down there.' Then she half rose, snatched the paper from my hands and slapped it down before the Revd. Micheldever. '*This* is in black and white. Every ratepayer in my Ward is livid at what is going on and how he is ruining the school Mr. Chadband built up painstakingly over the years! If he hasn't the grace to resign then we should sack him. And I move that.'

'The Inspectors' Report was quite good, in fact, very good,' the Vicar ventured.

'Oh them!' she cried. '*They* encourage it! It's what they learn at universities on the fat grants we fork out. But it's not them who have to live on top of it and has to pay for it. *They* can afford to be sloppy. You can be sure they send their kids to private schools.'

'It is all very difficult,' sighs the Vicar sounding distressed and picks up T. Fawcett's sad little document and studies it. 'What I can't understand is how a child living in the midst of the wonders of Nature, "the rushes by the water we gather every day, the tall trees in the greenwood, all things Bright and Beautiful" and so on, cannot see a Divine Hand at work. I expect his parents never brought him to the baptismal font. It is all very disappointing in a Christian country.'

'We should give him his cards now,' says Councillor Blossom. 'He has upset everybody. I have been talking to a great number of my ratepayers and they say all the teachers and children are up in arms about him and can't wait to see the back of him. How much notice do we have to give him, Mr. Tusker?' Tusker, to his credit, looked uncomfortable. 'I can pass on your wishes to the Director of Education,' he muttered. 'We can't do what you suggest at this level. It's a matter for the County Education Committee.'

'Well,' said Councillor Blossom triumphantly, 'we have County Alderman Tollemache on our side and we can rely on him to fix it at *that* end.'

By this time, being tittle-tattled over as if I was invisible, I was seething. In fact, I have not felt so affronted since Edith jilted me for her Glowsheen man, and I slapped the table with the flat of my hand and said in penetrating and sarcastic tones, 'For your information, in case you have not noticed, I *am* here! And I am not going to stay to listen to myself being walked over as if I am a paving-slab! In case you have forgotten (tempering my tone to one of irony), I have given Tampling twelve, repeat twelve years of loyal service and I have worked hard, and let

154

any of you deny that! And what do I get for twelve years teaching this Nation's Youth and Tampling's in particular? I get £50 in the bank, a bike and accessories and a couple of suits! You have not weighted me down with this World's Goods, have you? You do not pay me as much as a beauty salon rep!'

'You see what a vicious temper he has: he is not fit to be in charge of little children,' Councillor Mrs. Blossom interrupted. 'In fact, if you ask me, he is not even a Believer himself.'

'Oh, that can't be,' the Vicar exclaimed. 'Mr. Harpole was trained at one of our Church colleges. Furthermore this is a Church school. And he was reminding me of one of my own sermons only the other day . . .'

Mrs. Blossom looked narrowly at me and was going to let the matter drop but then had a new access of effrontery. 'I still say he's not a Believer,' she said flatly. 'Ask him!'

The Vicar said, 'I really don't think this is proper.'

'Well it's a Church school, you said so yourself,' the awful woman persisted. 'And you should never have left him in charge of it if he isn't a Believer.' She turned towards me again. 'Do you believe in God?' she shouted at me. 'And mind it's the Truth.'

'I used to believe in Her but now I have reservations,' I said, thinking how like Emma Foxberrow I sounded.

Even Alderman Tollemache came to life at that. In fact they all stared at me stupefied. Except the Blossom woman, who looked absolutely triumphant. 'There,' she said. 'What did I tell you, he doesn't believe in Nothing.' This annoyed me. 'I do,' I said firmly. 'I believe in the Holy Spirit which is also the Great Spirit of Freedom, this being resident in all of us,' adding (with a significant glance at Councillor Blossom) '. . . in larger or *lesser* degrees. And there is another thing I have come to believe in with increasing conviction this last term, and that is Hellfire and the Everlasting Pit.'

'And,' I went on, being now thoroughly up on my high horse, 'if all this brow-beating springs from that pathetic scrap of paper (indicating T. Fawcett's silly note) and, if I thought, like some of you, that God was a respectable, easily offended old gent with a permanently reserved hassock in the front pew, then I should join the Anti-Club myself to-morrow.'

Strangely, the Revd. Micheldever did not seem put out at all by this. 'Oh,' he said, 'that is a very interesting idea and I hope that you will develop it as I am deeply interested. For instance, would you be prepared to substitute the term "Holy Ghost" for "Holy Spirit", Mr. Harpole?'

I was about to be side-tracked into explaining that 'Ghost' had accumulated morbid connotations from Horror X films when Councillor Blossom shouted, 'I demand that my resolution sacking him be put to the meeting.'

This brought me back to the boil again and, directing a steady look at Tusker, I said heatedly, 'There are some who have licked boots for so long that they have developed a taste for being trodden on, and there are others (glaring at Councillor Blossom) who can only be happy when they have dragged some-one else into their troughs to wallow with them. If you really want to know what I believe, it is, "Time's meant for *dogs* and *apes*. Man has Forever." Browning ... And you need not cause yourselves further anxiety about my future as I am getting out of your broiler-house *now*. In fact, I shall leave it tomorrow and that is all the notice I am giving you.'

At this I pushed back my chair and stood up until County Alderman Tollemache told me to sit down again which I did.

'For once I have something else to say besides asking for an opinion on Percussion,' said Alderman Tollemache. 'And, whilst on that subject, do not suppose that I have been unaware of your supercilious sniggers over the years, but it seems to me to be no more stupid than the questions the rest of you ask candidates for teaching posts. In fact, whereas *your* questions are asked by a thousand school-managers of candidates who have answers already prepared, *my* unique enquiry goes off under them like a land-mine. I am thus able to assess Crisis Reaction whereas *you* are only able to obtain a Fawning Quotient.

'In fact, I well recall enquiring our friend Harpole's opinion of Percussion when he first came here as a young teacher. He did not descend to dissimilation: in fact, all he could do was gawp at me. From this I deduced – accurately so it seems – that he was stupid but straight-forward. Meanwhile, in sure and certain expectation, I await the Great Day when the Ideal Candidate will present himself and echo my own deeply felt conviction that Percussion is an unnatural noise wrung from children by teachers of debased sensibility and defective hearing.'

This impassioned declaration made a profound impression on

156

all, and I was reflecting on how I should enjoy repeating it (with one omission) to Emma Foxberrow, when he continued, 'But that is only by the way. I have here a letter relevant to the matter under discussion which I shall ask the Chairman to read aloud.' Which he did.

'We, the undersigned, desire to have it recorded that we have complete confidence in our colleague, Mr. G. Harpole and trust that his very successful period as acting-headmaster of this school will be noted by the Primary School Managers.'

Signed: Rita Grindle-Jones
Grace Tollemache
James Pintle
H. Croser.

I was flabbergasted and not a little conscience-stricken remembering certain episodes with all the signatories and bitterly regretted my lack of consideration over Croser's skull, Miss Tollemache's wreath and dear old Pintle's stubborn defence of the Old Maths.

'And,' went on the Alderman, 'contrary to Councillor Mrs. Blossom's malicious invention, I understand also that a letter has been sent by numerous rate-paying parents.'

He looked aggressively at Tusker who looked abashed and took a letter from his file.

'I should like to hear it, Mr. Chairman,' said the Alderman.

'This is from 147 parents represented by a Mr. and Mrs. Bull, Mr. and Mrs. Toseland, Mr. Fawcett, Mr. Widmerpool, Mrs. Widmerpool's sister, a Mr. Billitt and one who signs himself as "Alfred the Washerman",' said Tusker.

The Revd. Micheldever studied it for a few minutes.

'It begins with a very long declaration of the rights of parents under the 1944 Education Act, and a long extract from Section 17 of the Act. And, if I may be allowed to summarize, goes on to testify that, although several of the signatories may have engaged in controversy from time to time with Mr. Harpole, they recognize that the exchange of strongly held views is part of the democratic process.

'They then ask if Mr. Chadband could not be rewarded for his long years of unstinting service by making him an education officer and that Mr. Harpole be confirmed in his place.'

This letter (though naggingly familiar in tone) seemed so beyond the power of the ill-educated band who had signed it that I was not surprised when Tusker reluctantly added that it had come with a covering letter from a Mr. Alexander Festing.

The suggestion that Chadband be promoted with an expanded title to an area of diminished responsibility makes manifest that Festing is a clerical employee of some nationalized industry and well aware of the Peter Principle of Percussive Sublimation.

'Now,' said Alderman Tollemache. 'There is no need for me to ask if you share my feelings because I can see you do, so speaking for all here, I hope our friend Harpole will forget this little episode and give our school and the Tampling Cricket Club his sterling services for many a long season to come.'

There was a blast of loud Hear, Hears. (It sounded like clucking in the broiler-house.)

'Thank you,' I said (in dignified tones), 'but No. Because, since hearing a report of one of the Chairman's sermons and contrary to popular supposition, I have come to believe that *I* shall not live for ever and therefore intend to suit myself what I do for as long as my £50 holds out. In other words, it is enough for me to get on with the washing.'

This took them all aback.

'Perhaps you are right,' said Alderman Tollemache. 'Yes, perhaps you are right. But if you ever wish a head-mastership in this county you can rely on me absolutely. The password is *Percussion!*'

I then left the room.

25

To my surprise and great pleasure who should I find waiting for me outside the Office but Emma and Titus Fawcett. They listened to my story with immense interest and when I had done, Emma said, 'Well done!' 'Yes, Mr. Harpole, well done,' echoed Titus Fawcett. 'You have struck a notable blow for Liberty,' she went on ('Which shall never be put out', echoed the child). 'Give it a couple of years and even One-of-the-Old-School Pintle and the scarifying Grindle-Jones will return to grudgingly tell new staff, "Ah, that was in the Great Days, in Harpole's Time!" This is indeed a Glorious Victory – when the chips were on the table They found that one man could not be put down.'

'By "They", Miss Foxberrow means "Tyranny",' remarked Titus Fawcett.

'Ah,' I said, 'it is all right for you, here to-day and gone to-morrow. *I* had Career Prospects and look at them now – in ashes. I don't know what has happened to me. I did not used to be like this. I used to be looked up to.'

'Oh,' she said, looking amused, 'so you don't know what has been happening to you? Well, do not brood upon it. The Old Harpole is dead and a New Man is risen up. You have advanced back to your Glorious State of Original Sin. You have fought the Good Fight and have suitable scars to prove it.'

'Yes, that is all very well,' I interrupted, 'but how am I going to make a living. I am not by nature a loafer. What can I do?'

'Why,' she exclaimed, 'with the New Power stirring in your blood what can you not do! You can do Anything! But if you must go on teaching, then you must teach Liberty. God knows the fat, pampered and servile citizens of this once great land, solely preoccupied to increase its Gross National Product, the belly, can do with it.'

'Where are *you* going?' I asked. 'We could find another job together, perhaps in Barchester.'

'No,' she said firmly, 'I have planted my seed and Titus here will remain to nurture it. But you will need to exercise Subtlety and Discretion, Titus; in the Authoritarian State of English Education, a child is very vulnerable even with help from your Dad, for whose views on the value of purposeful illiteracy I have the greatest admiration.'

Then, turning back to me, she said somewhat smugly, 'I have been appointed Principal of the Central Missionary Society's Crash Course for teachers-in-training in Zanzambia.'

'A missionary!' I exclaimed. 'But you are not a Believer!'

'That is unimportant,' she replied. 'Neither is Croser, yet he will be Head of a Church school in the fullness of time. For me not to believe in the same god as the Archbishop of Canterbury has great advantages. Whereas *he* is bound to teach humility and prayer, I shall teach my Africans that all Good springs from Action – as you discovered yourself with Billitt.' She paused and raised her eyebrows. 'Your father has written that you should come and help me,' she said simply, 'the Field being as it were ripe unto harvest, (as he said) and the Labourers few.'

'Oh!' I exclaimed in utter bewilderment. 'But are you not going to marry Edward Muttler?'

'Certainly not,' she replied. 'He does not need me and I do not need him. Apart from gratifying his animality I can do nothing for him.'

'Will you marry me, Miss Foxberrow?' I said.

'No,' she answered (but very kindly). 'No, not at the moment. And you may call me Emma since last term's charade is now ended. You may sleep with me now and then and, if we fit and the work goes well, we could rationalize the arrangement for the sake of the children.'

Titus Fawcett had been listening to this with great attention and I quietly indicated this.

'Oh,' she said, 'do not slip back into your Old Ways: I have great confidence in this child and he might as well learn early as late that the Romantic Conception of Love is bunk. When he reaches puberty I shall not expect him to shackle himself to some stupid girl who can offer him nothing except domestic service, a double bed licensed by Society and a mother-in-law to visit on Sundays.'

Had a farewell rum with Shutlanger in The Fusilier as he is leaving the Grammar School to become a novitiate in an Anglican Monastery. His language was however as unrestrained as ever and he kept repeating that he was 'withdrawing from the b * * * * y world, surry'. He urged me to drop-in if ever I passed near his new address and said he would 'keep a billet warm for me' when I'd had enough of 'this education lark'.

I then asked him if, in his new vocation, he had forgiven his wife and the big Sixth-former, but his violent outburst regrettably demonstrated that he had not.

A most unexpected occurrence. At ten o'clock at night whilst we were studying a map of Zanzambia there was a knock on my sitting-room door and it was Mr. Tusker of all people. I looked hostilely at him since there was now nothing to lose, but he looked embarrassed and sheepish and asked if he might come in. I called, 'Here is an official, dear. Is it quite convenient for him to come in?' To my astonishment Emma replied loudly, 'Just give me time to put on my skirt.' Then I reluctantly invited him in and offered him a chair. A moment later Emma appeared from my bedroom ostentatiously smoothing back her hair whilst Tusker looked on with astonishment tinged with envy. 'Look here, Harpole,' he began nervously.

'*Mr.* Harpole,' Emma corrected him quite fiercely.

'Yes, *Mr.* Harpole,' he said. 'Look here, I'm awfully sorry about today. What happened, I mean. Some of the things which transpired were definitely not in order. In fact, I shall report the details to the Chief in the morning at the County Offices. In fact, if you will consent to withdraw your resignation, you can count on my support. *They* were *quite* out of order.'

'Oh!' I exclaimed, the wind taken out of my sails hearing this from Tusker who, after Councillor Mrs. Blossom, I had regarded as my bête noire.

'Yes,' he went on. 'As a matter of fact, I personally have been considerably impressed by your period as Acting Head of Tampling St. Nicholas and had strongly recommended you for favourable consideration by the Education Committee when next a suitable vacancy occurred.'

'Well,' I said to vigorous and encouraging nods from Emma,

'if that is so, you have been at considerable pains to conceal your high opinion.'

'I agree,' he said. 'And I feel rather badly about it, but you cannot imagine how difficult my position is, Mr. Harpole. Some of your colleagues seem to think that my sole function is to agree with *them* and to do whatever *they* want. And the Managers believe that I should always side with *them*. Then there are some parents who are most indignant if I do not immediately perform whatever *they* consider ought to be done for the sole benefit of their child. And *the Chief* always insists on having the final word and is not above over-ruling me. Believe me, my position is not easy. There are times when I wish that I had never left the form-room . . .'

He might well have developed this piteous theme but Emma briskly interrupted and told him what we had decided, which plainly amazed him. And, when he saw that there was no changing my mind, he wished us all success and said he hoped that I would always look on him as a friend. I found it hard to give credibility to this request but, despite Emma's raised eyebrows and an audible whistle of amazement, I shook hands and he went.

What can one say to all this? It leaves no doubt that Tusker, the professional local government officer would, in the breach, have put aside Tusker the querulous plantation overseer and (albeit grinding his teeth) would have prevented Harpole's dismissal. He would be well aware that the N.U.T., lately shaking itself from its hundred years' slumber, would bring up its lumbering resources into a fight which would not have left him (Tusker) unscathed. Furthermore the Revd. E.J. Micheldever, having to live on upon the battlefield, would not have allowed himself to be drawn irrevocably into this squalid affair.

And, of course, there is that growing band of Tampling St. Nicholas parents, ransomed souls emerging from the long Chadbandian night, ready aye ready to write anonymous letters to the Sentinel and harass the local politicians who periodically appear on their doorsteps begging votes.

But, of his free will, Harpole has resigned and now must pick up the fragments of a shattered career as best he can. Frankly, one does not feel called upon to cry Woe! Woe! This is not the Harpole

*who, with such hesitant heart, took his stand at the official wicket
three months ago. This is a new Harpole, Harpole Resurgent,
refined (one might venture to say) as gold in the furnace. In fact,
as Miss Foxberrow intuitively knew when she glimpsed him
through her screen of willows, a Harpole finally ready to outface
fate. With her to counsel, inspire and stiffen, to what heights might
he not rise?*

JOURNAL

For my final morning service in Assembly I chose:

> 'Through the night of doubt and sorrow,
> Onward goes the Pilgrim Band,
> Singing songs of Expectation,
> Marching to the Promised Land.'

As we sang the last line, Emma glanced significantly at me. With
her foot trod firmly on the loud pedal, Mrs. Grindle-Jones then
played us out to the Hyacinth Waltz.

Before leaving the old school for the last time I emptied my
drawers so that all is left ship-shape for Mr. Chadband's return.
After some thought decided to dispense Sir H. Newbolt's poem
into the waste-paper basket as I now perceive in it a facile
Greyfriars flavour which I used not to notice. Furthermore, I no
longer can subscribe to its sentiments. In my next post I shall
substitute the card which Emma gave me last night, this being
by J. Bunyan and very fine . . .

> 'And though with great difficulty I have gotten
> hither, yet now I do not repent me of all the
> trouble I have been at to arrive where I am.
> My sword I give to him who shall succeed me in my
> pilgrimage and my courage and skill to him that
> can get it. My marks and scars I carry with me
> as a sign that I have fought his battles who
> will now be my rewarder.
> So he passed over and all the trumpets sounded
> for him on the other side.'

> P.S. (in Emma's writing) For '*his*' battles
> read '*her*' battles. And you shall have your reward.
> E.F.

To-day relinquished charge of Tampling St. Nicholas C.E. (Aided) School.

HARPOLE TO SHUTLANGER (Much later)

... I am delighted to hear that you have made it up with your wife and are liking life in a village parsonage.

We are still at Sinji, once a wartime R.A.F. flying-boat station, each day disappearing a little more into the bush. There is a beachcomber who returned here after the War and we play cricket together on his sand-bar of an evening, with his wives doing the fielding. Emma is principal of our College and we are turning out surprisingly efficient teachers in 3 month crash-courses. Unfortunately I do not expect our college to be allowed to stay open. In fact, it probably will have shut down even before you receive this epistle. The circumstances being that a member of the Zanzambian Government visited on Graduation Day last week and his face became blacker as Emma exhorted our hundred students to cherish Freedom and resist Tyranny – if necessary, at the barricades.

The students venerate Emma and she will be long remembered in Africa. I am not married yet.

Bishop Wilton Lane,
The Yorkshire Wolds, 1971.

MORE ABOUT PENGUINS, PELICANS AND PUFFINS

For further information about books available from Penguins please write to Dept EP, Penguin Books Ltd, Harmondsworth, Middlesex UB7 0DA.

In the U.S.A.: For a complete list of books available from Penguins in the United States write to Dept DG, Penguin Books, 299 Murray Hill Parkway, East Rutherford, New Jersey 07073.

In Canada: For a complete list of books available from Penguins in Canada write to Penguin Books Canada Ltd, 2801 John Street, Markham, Ontario L3R 1B4.

In Australia: For a complete list of books available from Penguins in Australia write to the Marketing Department, Penguin Books Australia Ltd, P.O. Box 257, Ringwood, Victoria 3134.

In New Zealand: For a complete list of books available from Penguins in New Zealand write to the Marketing Department, Penguin Books (N.Z.) Ltd, Private Bag, Takapuna, Auckland 9.

In India: For a complete list of books available from Penguins in India write to Penguin Overseas Ltd, 706 Eros Apartments, 56 Nehru Place, New Delhi 110019.

Also published by Penguins

OH WHAT A PARADISE IT SEEMS
John Cheever

Skating on Beasley's Pond always makes Lemuel Sears feel nostalgic. He is old enough to wonder – after skating, or when he sees a young couple kissing in the cinema – whether sometime soon he will be exiled from the pleasures of love.

Meanwhile, there is Renée. He first noticed Renée, her style, her splendid and endearing figure, in a New York bank. With her, even in polluted, fast-food, nomad America, the illusion of Paradise lingers. Until he returns to find his free skating rink turned into a municipal dump. And until ... But Renée has always said, 'You don't understand the first thing about women.'

GINGER, YOU'RE BARMY
David Lodge

When it isn't prison, it's hell.

Or that's the heartfelt belief of conscripts Jonathan Browne and Mike 'Ginger' Brady. For this is the British Army in the days of National Service, a grimy deposit of post-war cynicism. The reckless, impulsive Mike and the more pragmatic Jonathan adopt radically different attitudes to this two-year confiscation of their freedom ... and the consequences are dramatic.

WISE VIRGIN
A. N. Wilson

Giles Fox's inexplicable failure to win a Fellowship at Kings, the unfortunate loss of two wives and now the onset of blindness have merely sharpened his resolve to astound the world with his interpretation of the Pottle manuscript, a little-known thirteenth-century tract on virginity.

But when Miss Agar, his academic helpmeet, impetuously proposes marriage, and when his daughter Tibba discovers the precocious and quite unmedieval charms of public schoolboy Piers Peverill, an intriguing new light is shed on Giles's investigations into the manuscript ...